POPPY'S
HERO

For Chloe, Phin, Raphael, Jacob, Claudio, Flora
and all the children with mums
or dads in prison

Text copyright © Rachel Billington 2012
The right of Rachel Billington to be identified as the author of this work
has been asserted by her in accordance with the Copyright, Designs and
Patents Act, 1988 (United Kingdom).

First published in Great Britain and the USA in 2012 by
Frances Lincoln Children's Books, 4 Torriano Mews,
Torriano Avenue, London NW5 2RZ
www.franceslincoln.com

A catalogue record for this book is available from the British Library.

ISBN: 978-1- 84780-192-0

Set in Palatino and AvenirLT

Printed and bound by CPI Group (UK) Ltd, Croydon, CR0 4YY
in November 2011

1 3 5 7 9 8 6 4 2

POPPY'S HERO

Rachel Billington

F

FRANCES LINCOLN
CHILDREN'S BOOKS

PART ONE

Heathrow Airport. London.

A big man with red curly hair is coming through the Customs Hall. He walks past the duty officers with a swagger. He even smiles a little. One of the officers beckons him over, crooking his forefinger.

The man freezes for a moment, then looks round as if he hopes they want someone else behind him.

The officer takes a step towards him. Two more officers appear from behind a screen. One is armed.

The man looks down at the large black suitcase he is pulling. There's another smaller case on top. He seems to have lost several inches in height and his smile has gone for good.

The three men close round him.

'Would you mind coming this way, sir.' It isn't a question.

Arriving passengers edge quickly past the little group, as if whatever the man has, might be catching.

The light in the hall is silver green and perhaps that is why the man's face has turned from ruddy pink to sickly grey. Or perhaps the light has nothing to do with it.

Chapter One

Poppy woke with flashing lights whirling round her head.

'Don't, Dad. I'm awake.' She opened her eyes to prove it and saw, first, the red and green lights in the glass globe, and then her mother's grey staring eyes, magnified by the glass.

'Where's Dad?' It was Dad – Big Frank – who had had the idea of holding the globe above her head to wake her up. He was like that. That's why she called him Big Frank. He was larger than life. Always having fun, trying to surprise. It felt silly when Poppy's mum tried to play games. Maybe being Polish meant she had a different sense of humour.

'Where's Big Frank?' Poppy knew her mum didn't like her using the nickname but she could never resist it.

'You know he's away.' Eyes and lights disappeared abruptly. 'Time to get up.'

Poppy's dad had been away for ages. It was only being asleep that made her forget. She called,

'When will he be back?' But her mum was out of the door.

Poppy pulled on her track-suit because it was gym day at school and rolled the rest of her uniform into a bag. Then she tinkled a bit on the piano, which was in her bedroom because there was nowhere else for it and Irena (that was her mother's name – not Irene like in English) was a piano teacher, so it had to be somewhere.

'Stop it, Poppy!' her mum shrieked from downstairs. She was easy to wind up, particularly first thing, particularly if someone messed with her beloved piano.

'Sorry.' Poppy knew she was being annoying because she missed Big Frank, which wasn't her mum's fault. At least, she supposed it wasn't her fault.

After this bad start, the day went on as usual. Poppy and her mum walked to school together and Poppy carried her bag without complaining and gave her mum a hug when she said goodbye.

Irena might be a bit different from other mothers, being Polish *and* musical, but she tried her best to do good. That's what Big Frank had said when Irena baked a cake for his birthday that looked and tasted like a cow pat.

'Your ma may not be a five star chef, but she's always trying to do good.' He'd raised Irena's arm in a victory salute, 'Your mother is that rare species, a GOOD WOMAN!' which Poppy thought well over the top. But that was her dad: pushing things to the limit.

'What are you smiling about?' Poppy's best friend, Jude, met her as they went into the locker room. Jude was short for Judith, which she didn't like because Judith had cut off the head of a man called Holofernes. In a story, of course. Privately, Poppy thought Jude was well capable of doing damage to an enemy, although she might think removing a head too messy. Jude was very neat.

'Nothing.' Poppy side-stepped Wimpy Will, who was as usual looking as if he might vomit. He was supposed to have some rare illness but no one was convinced. Jude had christened him Wimpy Will.

'I bet I can guess,' Jude persisted, her round brown eyes staring knowingly.

'Guess what?' asked Poppy, although she knew perfectly well.

'Why you're smiling.' Jude flicked her shiny pony- tail.

'How much?' asked Poppy.

'How much what?'

'How much do you bet?'

'A tube of wine-gums.'

'I don't like wine-gums.'

'Fruitellas?'

'I hate Fruitellas.'

'Rollos?'

'OK. So why was I smiling?'

'Because you were thinking of your dad!' Jude gave a honking laugh of triumph, then turned to go into assembly. Her springy, confident walk made her pony-tail swing.

Poppy followed. Thing was, everyone recognised her dad and he *did* make people smile – even Jude. Poppy and he shared the same red curly hair which made her proud, even though the hair itself was a nuisance. However much she brushed, it always escaped into wild tangles.

Her dad had been picking her up most days this summer and he always had some joke. One time, he'd been wearing hologram glasses which gave him goggly protruding eyes and made everyone scream with horrified laughter. Another time, he'd lined up all Poppy's friends, told them to open their mouths and tried to throw in chocolate peanuts. Miss Docherty had stopped that.

'You win, Jude,' said Poppy. 'Thinking about my dad did make me smile. But you'll have to wait for your money. I'm broke.'

Poppy and Jude were occasionally allowed to walk home together with no adult, and this was one of the days. Jude's parents both worked and Irena was sometimes teaching. Jude had two older brothers, Ben and Rico, who were in the senior school and quite often they linked up, although the girls pretended not to like it.

'Boys are *so* loud!' Jude liked to say, pursing her mouth, although Poppy knew she thought her brothers were wonderful. Ben was nearly six foot and he was only fifteen.

On this afternoon the boys caught them up and Ben shouted, 'You're like two snails crawling along.'

'And I suppose you're Gerard and Rooney,' called back Poppy.

There was no hurry, she thought, the sun was warm and it was nice to walk slowly, chatting about Ulrika's new disgusting spiky hair and the awful Will who lived nearby so there was always a danger of meeting him. 'Smelling of sick,' said Jude with relish.

It was a bit disappointing when Jude went home with her brothers but then, she always did just what she wanted. Her house had four floors and a garden and a huge trampoline.

That was the thing about being an only child: you had to make a plan if you wanted someone to do things with.

Poppy let herself into her house – they had just the ground and first floor – feeling a little sorry for herself.

'Poppy! Is that you? Poppy!'

It was a surprise to find her mother in the kitchen – quite frazzled too, by the sound of it. Who else would it be but her? Unless it was Big Frank. Now, that would be better news.

'It's me, Mum.'

Irena stood in the kitchen holding a cup of tea. She usually looked pretty with her slim figure, big eyes and shiny chestnut hair. Just now she looked dreadful. Her eyes were red like a ghoul and her face like puff pastry.

'What's the matter? asked Poppy. Not that she really wanted to know. Grown-ups always had something the matter and it was best to steer clear.

8

Jude said her mum had once thrown a plate at her dad which had missed him and made a dent in the wall behind. So then she'd circled the hole in red and written, 'There are limits.'

Jude said it was a clever way of getting the living room redecorated and her dad was Italian so he liked shouting, but her mum was the one who threw the plate because she was an activist. Poppy's parents never argued; the worst that happened was Irena getting at Big Frank, her Polish accent growing stronger and stronger. But Poppy only heard it at night through her bedroom wall.

'You're home early.' Poppy pulled her homework out of her bag on to the kitchen table and tried to avoid looking at her mum. She could sense her standing watching, not even drinking her tea.

Suddenly, her mum said in a strange loud whisper, 'He's not coming back.'

There was no way Poppy could avoid hearing this. 'What do you mean? Mum, what are you saying?' She felt her voice rising. She hadn't even asked *who* was not coming back. It was horribly obvious.

'Your dad.' Irena spoke in a dull voice now, then she sat down at the table wearily. 'Dad's not coming back.'

For a moment Poppy couldn't say a word. But the silence was terrifying. Poppy went over to the hunched figure of her mum and began to shout, 'Why don't you explain? Do you mean he's never coming back? Do you mean you're splitting up? You're *divorcing*?' She could only say the word because she knew it was impossible. It had to be impossible.

'No. No! Of course I don't mean that.' Irena's voice was louder now, and she looked at Poppy – which was better than sitting with her head bowed. 'He's just not coming back soon.'

'But how long? What does "soon" mean?' Although Poppy was still shouting, she felt tears at the back of her eyes.

'I don't know how long. I really don't.' Her mum was back to that strange loud whisper. Tears were trickling from her eyes, which for some reason made Poppy even crosser.

'I bet it's your fault!' she yelled. 'He's going because he wants to get away. . . She never finished the sentence because her mother took a step towards her, and slapped her face. Hard.

Poppy, completely shocked, stood holding her hand to her cheek.

Irena stared at her, horror-struck. 'I'm sorry! Oh, everything is bad. But never, never say he not wants me.'

Sobbing, she ran from the room and up the stairs to her bedroom.

➤⭐➤

Poppy sat down and put her head in her hands. Her cheek was still hurting. Probably it was bright red. She thought vaguely that she was a little girl and that her mum loved her and her dad loved her – so what had happened?

She replayed their voices in her head, hers angry, her mum's miserable – until she'd lost her temper and flown at her. Her mother never lost her temper.

Poppy didn't understand. Everything was horrible and she couldn't even ring Jude because, although she was her best friend, she could never ever tell her what her mum had done. Her mum *loved* her. They *loved* each other. Oh, why was everything so bad? Bad. BAD. And where was her father?

Too shocked to cry or to do her homework, even though she had an essay to write on a subject she really enjoyed, Poppy shut her eyes and did absolutely nothing.

After about an hour, her mother came quietly into the room and stood beside her. Poppy turned round and looked at her as if she was a stranger. She noticed her mum had a scared expression on her face, as if she'd seen a ghost.

'I never forgive myself,' she whispered. 'I am so very sorry, my darling Poppy. My darling, special daughter. Flower girl, my own lovely Poppy.'

For a moment Poppy thought of all the mean things she could say, like, 'Your priest will forgive you in confession, won't he?' or, 'You're not fit to be a mum!' or even, 'I hate you!' But the truth was, she wanted all this horribleness to be over and to be back where they were before.

'Oh, Mum! I'm so sorry for shouting at you.' Poppy flung herself into Irena's arms and they stayed like that for a long time, just hugging and feeling safe together.

When they separated, Irena began to make supper more slowly than usual – no singing, which she often did, but still, things seemed back to normal. Of course, they weren't really.

As Poppy took out her homework, she began

to think all over again: where is my dad? What is the story about Big Frank?

She looked at Irena's back. Dare she ask her?

'You like grated cheese over your baked beans?' asked Irena, half-turning. Her voice was all quavery.

No, decided Poppy, I'm definitely not going to ask her tonight. Maybe in the morning. Or maybe she'll tell me.

Then it struck her that perhaps her mum really didn't know, and that was the most frightening thought of all.

The man has handcuffs holding his big hands tight together. He looks dazed, as if he can't believe where he is or what's happening to him.

Around him, the business of the court goes on but he hardly hears it.

The man in charge of things makes a pronouncement and from one of the benches, a woman with soft chestnut hair and big grey eyes shouts, 'No! No!'

The big man doesn't even look in her direction. He stares at his lap and seems to shut his eyes for a moment.

Then he's taken away again. A burly policeman holds him on either side. The whole event has hardly taken more than a few minutes.

Chapter Two

A week passed and it was another Monday, and Poppy still didn't know what had happened to her dad.

The hot sunny spell had broken and it was drizzling a little but she didn't mind that. All her favourite lessons were on Monday and she didn't object when Will tagged along on the walk to school, nor even mind when Jude went into assembly without waiting for her.

'Hi, Jude,' she called, and was a little surprised when Jude ignored her and went into a huddle with a group of other girls.

At break, when they were all in the playground – it had stopped raining and it felt good to be outside the stuffy building – Jude did come over.

'Good weekend?'

'We went up to Hampstead Heath to see the kites.'

'With your dad, were you?' asked Jude, with a sunny smile on her face. There was something

15

altogether odd about her expression, Poppy thought, sort of sly and excited.

'He's not back yet,' said Poppy, uncomfortably. 'He's abroad, working.'

'Oh, yes.' Jude's voice had a nasty jeering tone, as if she knew a secret.

At this point Tania joined them. She was a gentler girl than Jude – Poppy tended to think her boring. Now she just looked embarrassed.

'Have you told her we know?' asked Tania softly to Jude but loud enough for Poppy to hear.

'I'm just trying to find out if she knows,' answered Jude, staring at Poppy, 'and I don't think she does. Or else she's a very good liar.'

'That's so bad!' exclaimed Tania, looking even more embarrassed. 'Why don't we just drop it, then.'

'What do you mean?' demanded Poppy. She hated the look on Jude's face, who was supposed to be her friend, and now silly Tania seemed to be trying to protect her.

Another girl from their group, a sporty girl called Amber, came over to them. She wore the same embarrassed look as Tania.

'Tell me!' commanded Poppy. She had always been

a leader among her friends. She and Jude, top dogs, good at work, lots of go. She'd never felt like this before, with girls like Tania and Amber almost looking as if they were sorry for her.

'Oh, leave it,' said Amber. 'The bell will ring any minute, anyway.'

'But I think she should know.' Jude looked at Poppy thoughtfully. 'Do you want me to tell you?'

Poppy felt her heart hammering against her ribs and her mouth dry as dust. 'Yes,' she whispered.

Jude took a deep breath, 'Your dad is in prison. In prison,' she repeated louder. She looked up, her dark eyes bright. 'That's where your wonderful hero dad is: in prison!'

Then the bell for the end of break rang.

Somehow Poppy had to get through the rest of the day.

At lunch, she avoided all her friends and went to sit on her own. Of course, she didn't believe a word Jude had said, but she needed to work out why she'd said it and what it was all about.

She was staring at her fish and chips, knowing

she couldn't manage a bite, when Will came over.

'Can I sit here?'

Poppy moved over to give him room. He didn't seem to know anything, although he must have wondered why she wasn't sitting with her usual friends. She looked at his narrow face with the fair hair falling over his hazel eyes, and suddenly he seemed like the one person she could talk to honestly.

She pushed away her food. 'Jude and the others say my dad's in prison. Wherever could they have got such a stupid idea?'

'Oh.' Will stared down at his lunch box and Poppy saw he'd gone bright red.

'It's obviously totally stupid,' she repeated to herself. 'I just can't think why Jude would make up something like that.' She looked at Will appealingly. Why didn't he say anything?

He closed the lid of his box. 'I'm sorry,' he said, not looking at her and still scarlet. 'It must be a horrible feeling.'

Poppy pushed her chair back and stood up. Without saying anything more, she hurried to the toilets and locked herself in. She thought she was going to be sick.

After a few minutes, she heard voices by the basins.

'I think she came in here,' said Tania.

'I suppose she wants to be alone,' said Amber.

'Then perhaps we'd better go,' said Tania, sounding relieved.

Poppy heard their footsteps going away. She decided to stay locked in until the bell rang for lessons. Why did people invent such horrible things? It almost looked as if Jude was jealous of Big Frank. Tears pricked in her eyes; one ran down her cheek. Grabbing a piece of toilet paper, she brushed it away angrily.

~ ~ ~

Even that long school day had to come to an end. Poppy stood waiting for her mum outside the school gates; she hadn't felt so keen to see her for months – years. Even if her mum couldn't be Big Frank, she knew she loved her. She would put things right.

The sun was shining brightly and Poppy rubbed her eyes which were sore from crying earlier. Well, she wouldn't be so feeble again.

Out of the dazzle, she saw Jude approaching.

How did she dare! Poppy thought. If Jude had any sense, she'd stay well out of her way.

But Jude kept on coming. Poppy saw she had a newspaper in her hand. When did any of them read a newspaper?

Poppy stood her ground. She wasn't going to run away from her so-called best friend. She did wish her mum would come. Her legs had begun to tremble.

'Hi,' said Jude. Her face still looked odd, although more anxious now, less cocky.

'Hi,' said Poppy.

'I thought I should be the one to tell you,' said Jude, her voice a bit hoarse. 'I know you'll think I'm mean, but soon everyone will know except you, and you wouldn't want that.'

Poppy stared at her, then at the paper. 'Why have you bought that?'

'Because you didn't believe me. Rico saw it over the weekend. He showed me.'

'Give it to me!'

Jude held out the newspaper. Poppy snatched it away and turned her back. She looked down. The paper had been folded to page five. There was a photo, not very big, of a smiling, curly-haired man. It was Big Frank, taken some years earlier.

Poppy read what was written underneath: *Arrested at Heathrow airport.*

'Poppy! Poppy!' Poppy heard her mother's voice as if in a dream. *Charged and held on remand in Her Majesty's Prison, Grisewood Slops.*

'Darling, I'm so sorry I'm late.'

Silently, Poppy held out the paper to her mother. Now her hands were trembling too.

Chapter Three

Irena took the newspaper and quickly folded it away in her handbag.

'No need for that,' she said decisively.

They started the walk home all on their own, as if everyone had decided they had an infectious disease. Poppy felt very hot and sweat trickled down her face and back.

After a few moments, Irena opened her bag again and offered Poppy a swig of water. For a second, Poppy caught sight of her dad's face again and the water went down the wrong way.

Irena patted her back. When the bottle was put away, she said, 'We talk about it when we get home.'

'All right.' Poppy felt too confused and miserable to object.

'Let's go in here,' said her mum the moment they'd opened the front door. She pointed to the little sitting-room crowded with boxes and papers from her dad's work where they almost never sat. Poppy thought it was like going into the headmaster's study.

'Yes,' said her mum, frowning from the sofa – Poppy was perched uncomfortably on a little stool. 'Your father is in prison.'

'But Mum. . .' interrupted Poppy. Irena held up her hand in a rather foreign way she had. Sometimes Poppy couldn't help wishing she had an English mother who spoke without an accent. Irena couldn't even pronounce 'father' properly.

'Please. I finish first. Now I see I should tell you. You are too old for it to stay secret. I am very, very sorry. You are quite right to be angry.'

Poppy tried to think if she was angry. She had been before, when she didn't know anything, but now she just felt anxious and unhappy. Why was her dad in prison? Arrested at Heathrow, like the paper had said. Her mum had taken it away before she'd read any more.

'I suppose it's a mistake,' she said miserably. She thought what she needed most was a big hug, but the person she most wanted to give it wasn't here. Her mother, on the other hand, had a distracted, non-hugging look about her.

'I suppose that is so.' Irena's voice was stiff. 'He is in prison. Although not convicted. You understand that?'

'Not really.'

'He has not been found guilty,' said her mum.

'Of course he's not guilty!' cried Poppy. 'But if he's not guilty, why's he in prison?'

'I know. I know. Your English law is very bad. They like locking people up even when they're innocent.' Poppy saw her mum's lower lip was trembling as if she was about to cry.

'He'll get out, then, when they realise they've got it wrong,' she said hastily.

'Your dad's a *good* man,' said Irena, 'but sometimes he does things without thinking. Some of his friends are not so very good.'

'Then people get the wrong idea,' said Poppy, trying to understand. What she did understand was that her mother thought Big Frank was innocent, and she thought that it must be true because up to this last week her mum had always been a very truthful person.

'I'll tell you what,' said her mum, pulling herself up and making the effort to be bright and bustling. 'I cook all your favourite things for tea.'

Without waiting for an answer, she hurried to the kitchen.

Poppy realised the conversation about her dad was finished and in a way she wasn't sorry.

'Take some money from my bag,' called her mum, 'and buy a couple of Mars Bars.'

So it was to be a rice pudding and Mars Bar sauce. It seemed odd after what they'd been talking about. Guilty and not guilty. Innocent, like her dad.

Poppy walked slowly to the corner shop. The sun was still warm. It was a beautiful evening when people expected to have a nice time and be happy. But how was she supposed to feel, when her dad was in some horrible prison cell which she couldn't even really imagine? He wouldn't be eating rice pudding and Mars Bars sauce.

The shop was crowded, so Poppy didn't notice Jude immediately – then she saw she was hiding at the end of one of the aisles.

'Two Mars Bars, please, Zita.' Poppy paid her money and marched out of the shop. The alternative was to go over and slap Jude hard. If Jude wanted to play it this way, then she wasn't going to go begging for her company. All the same, she had a sad, lonely feeling. How was she going to cope, with no one to talk to?

Some time between six and seven, when Poppy had gone up to her bedroom feeling rather sick after all the tea she'd eaten to please her mum, the doorbell rang.

Poppy jumped off the bed and stood by her door, heart pounding. Wildly, she imagined her dad standing outside, all this silliness forgotten, his big presence and loud voice filling their flat. Then she realised he would have let himself in, so instead, she imagined two policemen had come to tell them – but there her imagination failed her. Perhaps they'd tell them that Big Frank would be let out tomorrow.

'Poppy!' her mother called from below, 'Will's come to see you.'

Poppy's first thought was not to go down. Why would she want to see Will? He wasn't even a proper friend. On the other hand, he would be someone to talk to, and anything was better than lying around worrying.

'Send him up!' she shouted.

Will came into the room, looking surprised. 'You've got a piano in your bedroom!' he said.

'My mum *is* a piano teacher,' replied Poppy. It felt good to be a little sharp.

'It's nice,' said Will. 'Gives a special atmosphere. Do you play?'

'Like an elephant plays. I'm a disappointment to my mum.'

'Join the club,' said Will, sitting on the piano stool. 'My mum would like me to be the sort of fit and healthy person who plans to climb Everest.'

There was a silence. Poppy hesitated. She looked at Will's pale face with its high forehead overhung by a lock of beige-coloured hair. Perhaps it was because he had his own problems – always had, she supposed – but he seemed more sympathetic than any of her friends.

'I've talked to my mum,' she said, 'about my dad.'

'Oh, yes.' Will looked away, blushing a bit. He didn't have that horrid sly look she still remembered from when Jude had come up to her.

'It is true. He is in prison. But he's innocent. They're just keeping him there until he can prove it.'

'I *thought* he was innocent,' said Will, and this time Poppy found herself blushing too, but with pleasure, not embarrassment. 'He's so great,' continued Will. 'My dad left home when I was two. My mum says it was when I was having my big operation. You're lucky to have such a great dad.'

'*I* think so!' Poppy found she was smiling, actually smiling! 'He shouldn't be in prison at all.'

'Certainly not,' agreed Will, looking serious. 'I suppose we could try and get him out.'

'What?' Poppy, who'd been lounging on the bed, sat upright.

'You know, help him escape.' Will's voice rose. 'The other day I watched a TV film about prisoners of war escaping from a great moated castle in the middle of nowhere. It was called *Colditz*. If they can do that, then surely we can get your dad out of Grisewood Slops. I suppose he is in Grisewood Slops?'

Poppy, who hadn't really thought about it, remembered that the name in the newspaper had been Grisewood Slops. 'Yes, I think so.'

'Well, it's only along the road. Not far.' said Will, sounding more and more excited. 'I've seen it from the number 745 bus. I mean, it's not in the middle of a wild moorland or something.'

Poppy tried to take in the idea that her dad wasn't in some remote unimaginable place but near a number 745 bus stop. A vague memory stirred. 'Isn't it somewhere near the hospital?'

'Yes. That's why I know it. I've spent more time in

that hospital than at home. At the back of the prison there are playing fields. Anyone can go there.'

'Oh!' was all Poppy could think of to say. Here was quiet, shy, 'Wimpy' Will filled with all sorts of info and positive planning. 'He shouldn't be held captive,' she said a bit feebly.

'No. That's what I think.'

'Do you seriously believe we can get him out?'

'Those POWs dug tunnels, climbed over roofs and some of them even built a glider plane in an attic nobody knew about. And they were in danger of being shot by the Nazis. At least nobody would shoot us.'

'No,' agreed Poppy a little doubtfully. She'd been taken to the House of Commons. The policemen outside had looked a fearsome lot with nasty big guns. On the other hand, it felt so much better to be involved in a plan rather than lying on her bed feeling miserable.

'So, what do you think?' asked Will.

'I'm on for it!' shouted Poppy, and as she spoke, she was filled with such a rush of energy that she jumped off the bed. 'So where do we start? Mapping the place, I'd say. After school tomorrow. We'll need pens, a ruler, a hard-backed pad.'

'Poppy!' called Irena from downstairs. 'Have you done your homework yet?'

'In a moment,' lied Poppy. How important was homework, when you were involved in a rescue plan to spring your dad from prison?

The big man stands in the middle of his small cell. He is waiting to be unlocked so he can go and have a shower. He has a small towel and a bar of soap held to his chest.

Behind him, his cell-mate lies half asleep on his bunk.

'They like keeping you waiting,' he says in a weasly voice.

The big man doesn't bother to answer, as if he doesn't care what his cell-mate thinks.

Clumping footsteps approach from outside the cell. A key is inserted in the lock and noisily turned. The big man stares at the door as if it holds some secret.

The heavy door is pulled slowly open. A man in white shirt with epaulettes and dark trousers looks in. He frowns at the weasly-voiced man, then inclines his head towards the big man. Clearly, he can't be bothered to speak.

The big man comes out of the cell and walks down the green corridor.

Chapter Four

'I'm going home with Will,' Poppy told her mother the next morning.

Irena looked surprised. She was also surprised that Poppy seemed quite cheerful, ate a huge bowl of cereal, then took a banana and some biscuits.

'In case I'm hungry at break,' she explained airily.

She and Will had it all worked out. After school, they'd catch the number 745 bus and go and do a recce on the prison. They'd obviously need extra supplies to eat. Poppy felt quite sorry for her mum, who was all sad and hopeless and wasn't trying to *do* anything. Grown-ups were like that, she thought, good at seeing the gloomy side and useless at taking positive action. In her back-pack she had a pad of paper and a fine pen she'd found in the living room. 'We've got to do this thing professionally,' Will had said, and she agreed. Big Frank's happiness was at stake.

With all this on her mind, Poppy wasn't worried

about school or how Jude and the other girls might behave. So she was surprised when Jude sidled up to her in break.

'Sorry,' she said.

'That's OK,' replied Poppy automatically.

But it wasn't OK. Jude had let her down when she needed her most and now she had other fish to fry.

Poppy moved away.

The less good moment was when the class were asked to hand in their homework and she hadn't done hers.

'Poppy?' questioned Miss Bavani, who was quite young and wore surprisingly trendy T-shirts.

'Sorry, Miss,'

'Sorry, meaning you haven't done it, or sorry, meaning you don't feel like handing it in?' Miss Bavani was being sarcastic but not really cross, because Poppy was one of her best students and was never late with her homework.

'Sorry, because I didn't do it because I wasn't feeling well.' Well, that was true enough.

'Don't let it happen again.'

'No, Miss.' Poppy caught sight of Will, who was giving an under-the-table thumbs up.

After that the day went on as usual, although

Poppy felt her excitement growing every minute. She and Will had agreed to slip away separately from the school gates and meet at the bus stop.

Poppy was first and she watched Will arrive, noticing his skinny body and laboured breath. He didn't look like a daring adventurer. But then, she supposed she didn't either.

It was an overcast, warm day and both decks of the bus were crowded and stuffy. Luckily Poppy and Will found two seats together on top at the back.

'It's six or seven stops,' said Will, sounding nervous.

'OK.' Poppy felt her heart pounding and thought, if they were both so tense when all they were doing was looking at the prison, what would they be like when they were actually trying to get her dad out?

'Oh. That's it!' cried Will suddenly. Poppy peered across him and saw a row of small grey houses and then tall gates and two tall towers.

They piled down the stairs. But it was too late. They'd missed the bus stop.

'Never mind,' said Will, as they finally got out. 'From here, we'd be best going round the back of the prison first.'

'Good idea,' agreed Poppy, who'd found the sight of the gates and towers and walls frightening, although of course she wasn't going to show it. 'I've often been past here,' she added, 'but never noticed the prison before. Now my dad's inside and it's as if he's invisible too.'

But Will wasn't listening. 'I think it's this way,' he said, pointing.

It wasn't easy to get to the back of the prison. The high walls with their rolls of barbed wire on top were easy enough to see, but they had a network of small houses and roads all around them.

'Are you sure there's a park at the back?' asked Poppy.

'Definite,' said Will. 'I've been there.'

'I wouldn't want to live so close to a prison,' said Poppy, as they went down yet another dead end with little houses on either side.

'Probably the people who live here work at the prison.'

'But these houses look quite ordinary,' said Poppy as they passed a garden filled with pots of red and white geraniums.

'Well, I suppose some quite ordinary people work there,' Will answered irritably.

Poppy was sure prison wardens were a special kind of person with dark, cruel faces but she didn't argue because she felt sorry for Will, who looked very tired and sweaty and was walking slower and slower. She was pretty hot herself. At last they saw greenery – green trees, green grass and even a bench.

'Phew!' exclaimed Poppy. Both of them flopped down and Poppy got out her bananas and biscuits and Will added two cartons of fruit drinks.

Once they'd revived, they looked around them.

'It's a big park,' said Poppy. Beyond the park she could see what looked like a sports stadium. Above their heads, birds tweeted in the big trees and a streaky sun came through the clouds 'Where's the prison?'

'Behind you,' said Will, smiling.

Poppy twisted round, and gasped. The high, dark walls of the prison were only a few metres behind them. Still holding half a banana, she stood up and stared. The walls looked very, very solid and there were towers at intervals, like she'd seen in a war movie.

'And they have dogs patrolling too,' said Will.

'There are lots of different buildings behind the walls,' Poppy said. 'We'll have to find which one Dad's in.'

While she was staring, Will took her pad and pen and started mapping out the prison. Then he drew in a little figure waving out of a window.

'That's Big Frank!' Poppy exclaimed.

'I love drawing figures, and your dad's so great. Larger than life. Always ready for a laugh. Do you remember when he took out a pound coin from Jude's nose?'

Both of them laughed, remembering the horrified expression on Jude's face as Big Frank shouted, 'I've never seen such a big bogey!'

'We *will* get him out, won't we?' Poppy asked quietly.

'Of course,' answered Will.

After that, they walked back round the prison again but this time the other way, and found they could follow the walls all the way.

Will did lots more drawings with more Big Franks on top of turrets and dancing along walls.

'You're *so* clever!' said Poppy happily, and they both felt so pleased with themselves that when they reached the main road and saw a bus coming along, they decided to try and catch it. The front of the prison could wait for another time.

'Operation Great Escape has begun!' said Poppy

exultantly, as they fell into their seats.

'Cheers!' cried Will, trying to give a high five but, as the bus gave a lurch at exactly that moment, their hands missed and they narrowly avoided tipping on to the floor.

Just for a moment Poppy caught a glimpse of the prison, making her mouth go dry, then she began giggling again. What was it her dad used to say: 'Faint heart never won Fair Lady'? In this case, the 'Lady' was a man, but she and Will had hearts like lions.

Chapter Five

Home was gloomy. Poppy didn't have to tell lies about what she and Will had got up to, because her mum had gone to bed with a headache.

In the end, she ate the ham sandwiches left out for her in front of the television and went to bed. Prison reccying certainly took it out of you.

The next morning Irena was up early. She sat watching Poppy eat her cereal.

'What is it, Mum? Poppy asked. Her mum never usually sat down with her.

'I saw your dad yesterday.' Irena's voice was strangled, as if she could hardly bear to say the words.

Poppy felt herself go as scarlet as her hair and her mind whirled. Her mum had *seen* Big Frank? Inside prison? Behind those walls that she and Will had studied so carefully? She thought of Will's drawings of the cheery man waving his arms out of a window, dancing along the walls.

Then another thought struck her: could her mum have been inside the prison at the same time she and Will had been walking round the outside? They might even have bumped into each other! 'What time did you see Dad?' she asked nervously.

Her mum looked surprised. 'One thirty.'

Poppy breathed a sigh of relief. 'Was he all right?' Her mind was racing. If her mum had been inside, she'd know which of the buildings Big Frank was in.

'I took him some books,' said Irena, 'but I wasn't allowed to give them to him. They said they were a security risk. Books!'

'Oh,' said Poppy, who was still trying to think straight.

'He sent you his love.'

Poppy pushed away her bowl abruptly. Her dad shouldn't be 'sending' his love, he should be here now, giving her a hug, joking about her hair sticking up like a frightened porcupine.

Toppling back her chair, she ran from the room and upstairs. 'Poppy!' called her mum in an unnatural voice that made her sound like an old lady.

'Don't worry, I'm coming,' Poppy called back angrily.

It was only as she went through the school gates that she realised she hadn't done her homework again. Trouble ahead, she thought dismally – then furiously. Why should she be expected to do homework when her dad was in prison! No one else's dad was in prison.

It was only meeting Will at lunch break that changed her mood. When she told him about her mum seeing her dad, he said immediately, 'So, can you visit him too?'

Poppy was taken aback. 'Mum didn't suggest it. She just said he sent his love – as if I was some remote cousin or something.'

'Why don't you ask her?'

Poppy wondered how to answer. When it came down to it, did she really want to see her wonderful dad in prison?

She was saved from answering by Jude and Tania brushing past.

'You look like two conspirators,' said Jude, nudging Tania and laughing.

It was true, Poppy thought, they look fairly silly huddled together among the coat hooks and lockers. It was a pity Will looked such a loser, when in fact he was really clever and daring.

'What's it to you?' was all she could think of to say.

The two girls went off chanting 'Wimpy Will' under their breath.

'Sorry,' said Poppy to Will.

'I'm used to it,' he said in a stiff voice.

'Sorry,' said Poppy again, remembering guiltily how she used to make fun of him. 'Anyway, I *will* ask Mum about visiting Big Frank. That's a very good idea.'

She only said it to make Will feel better, and he immediately brightened. 'Then you can pinpoint exactly where he is, which will make Operation Great Escape much easier.'

'OK,' said Poppy, who was already regretting her promise. 'I'll ask Mum tonight.'

'Another thing,' said Will. 'I think you should be nicer to Jude and the rest. Otherwise, they'll get suspicious about what we're up to.'

'I'll think about it,' said Poppy, who was beginning to think that Will was getting just a bit too bossy. The trouble was, he tended to be right!

The evening didn't begin well. Poppy had to hand over a letter from school telling her mum she hadn't been doing her homework. But to her surprise, Irena wasn't cross,

'Never mind, my darling. You've always been a top student.'

'Yes,' said Poppy doubtfully. She'd liked school before – it had been so easy. Now she didn't likeanything.

'Tonight we are having fun,' continued Irena. 'Look what I have bought.' She took a music book from her bag and flourished it in front of Poppy. 'All your favourite hits.' She turned the cover so that Poppy could see. 'Now we will go upstairs and I will play to you. Such fun we will have!'

Poppy followed her upstairs slowly. She felt like crying – again. She mustn't let it become a habit. It was so pathetic, her mum trying to make her happy by playing songs. Didn't she realise that hits from *Annie* or *The Phantom of the Opera* or *Cats* were oldies' stuff? Anyway, she knew her mum really only liked classical music. But they both spent an hour pretending to have a nice time and it was a warm feeling to be together.

Over spinach pancakes – a Polish favourite –

Poppy gathered her courage before she said in a bright tone, 'Maybe I could come with you next time you go and see Dad?' She stared at her mother, who looked so taken aback that she added quickly, 'I mean, I haven't seen him for ages.' This was such a silly thing to say that she had to stifle a hysterical laugh. Of course she hadn't seen him for ages – because he was in PRISON!

'I don't know.' Irena sounded anxious. 'I didn't think you'd want to come.' She paused. 'I don't know that your papa would like you to see him in a place like that.'

It was always a sign that Irena was upset when she referred to Poppy's dad as 'Papa', as if he were her own papa back in Poland.

Poppy hadn't thought what it would be like to visit her dad in a cell, like visiting a tiger in the zoo, all caged up. She'd never liked zoos.

She couldn't tell her mum the real reason for wanting to see her dad: so that she and Will could plan their Operation Great Escape better.

'I just thought it would be nice,' she said feebly.

'Nice,' echoed Irena doubtfully.

Picturing the walls and towers and barbed wire of the prison, Poppy decided that 'nice' was unlikely to be the right word.

'Good,' she said.

'I'll ask him.' Irena made an effort to sound cheerful again. 'Now, eat up, before the pancakes go cold.'

Poppy did as she was told. Then she did her homework, but not at all well because she kept thinking about going inside those high, dark walls.

That night she woke up suddenly, heart racing, eyes staring into the blackness. She'd been dreaming she was locked in a tiny room at the top of a tall tower attached to a castle, and everyone else was asleep so they couldn't help her. It was a bit like the story of the Sleeping Beauty, except that there was no knight to come and rescue her.

Usually, after a bad dream, she'd have gone to her mum's room, but Mum would always ask her to describe the dream and Poppy didn't want to tell her this one. So instead, she lay quietly until dawn came soft and friendly through the curtains.

Chapter Six

Poppy was in trouble at school. But she didn't care.

'I'll have to send you to the headmaster if it goes on like this,' said Miss Bavani. She twisted a bangle on her arm. 'I just don't know what's got into you.'

Jude and some of the girls who did know giggled at this, but Poppy just looked sulky.

'I used to be able to rely on you to work properly and bring your homework in on time.' Miss Bavani sighed regretfully. 'You'd better see me at the end of the day. You are still in junior school.'

'Yes, Miss.' What did Poppy care? What difference did school, junior or senior, make to anything that mattered?

But Irena frowned when she brought home yet another letter from school.

'Oh, Poppy,' she said sadly.

'Did you ask Dad?' Poppy frowned. How could her mum pretend that anything was normal? 'About my visiting him?' she added fiercely, in case there could be any doubt.

'Your dad was shocked you wanted to see him. He wanted to spare you such a sight. But I said you were old enough to know your mind, and after all, other kids visit. So he agreed that if you truly want to, you may go, even though he doesn't really think it's a good idea.'

'But does he *want* to see me?' cried out Poppy, before reminding herself that wasn't the point. The point, as Will kept telling her, was to get him *out*.

'Of course, my darling!' Irena shot up and held Poppy in her arms. 'He *loves* you!'

Held tight in her mum's arms, Poppy shut her eyes for a moment. 'I would like to see him,' she whispered into her mum's warm neck.

'Then we will arrange it, I expect, on Saturday.'

Will was very pleased when Poppy told him the news.

'Maybe I could stand outside the walls and you could wave,' he suggested enthusiastically.

Even Poppy could see that was a pretty unlikely scenario. 'You really think I could open a window in a prison and stick my head out?'

'I don't see why not.' Will made a cross face. 'You've got to breathe, haven't you.'

'There is such a thing as air conditioning,'

It was a stupid thing to argue about. Both of them knew that. It was just nerves.

'I've probably read too many adventure stories,' admitted Will. 'One year I was in hospital or at home for nearly six months, so all I did was read or draw.'

'Poor you,' said Poppy. They were sitting on a wall in the playground and, looking at Will in the bright sunlight, she was struck by how frail he seemed. 'Are you all right now?'

'Oh, yes. The doctors are keeping an eye on me. And no contact sports.'

At the other end of the playground a noisy group of boys and girls were playing a kind of touch football. Poppy watched them dashing about and couldn't help thinking what fun they were having while she sat there with Will, both of them so serious.

'You'd like to be with them, wouldn't you?' said Will, following where she was looking.

'Not after how Jude behaved.' Poppy turned back to Will.

'Do you think she told lots of people? About your dad, I mean.'

'What do I care!' Poppy tossed her head scornfully. 'Anyway, it's none of their business. The main thing is, he's innocent,' she added.

'That's why we're getting him out,' Will said soothingly.

But Poppy was too upset to stay still. She went to the toilets and locked herself in until she'd recovered.

That afternoon they had double science, but Poppy was so distracted that she got into trouble again.

'You're just not trying, Poppy. I'm very disappointed in you,' said Mr O'Donovan. Usually she was one of his favourites.

'Sorry, Miss,' said Poppy mechanically, and everyone laughed. Which didn't make Mr O'Donovan any happier.

It was a relief when the day came to an end and her mum was there to meet her. However, she looked flustered, with two bright spots of colour on her cheeks.

'What is it, Mum?' Poppy just stopped herself from asking, 'What's wrong, now?' Because that's how it felt – one bad thing after another.

They walked a little way before Irena spoke. 'I'm afraid I've done something you won't like, Poppy.'

'What?'

'I know it's the right thing. Your dad didn't like it either.'

'What?' repeated Poppy anxiously.

'I talked to your headmaster about your dad.'

'You've told Mr Hannigan!' Poppy grabbed her mother's arm.

'They needed to understand the problem. Why your work might suffer.'

'But now everyone will know!'

'No, no. He'll just tell the teachers who need to know. . .'

'Half the school knows already,' Poppy interrupted, 'after Jude brought in that newspaper.'

'She shouldn't have.' Now it was her mum's turn to look upset. 'Why did she, I wonder? Your best friend. . .'

'Because she's a horrible stupid ugly pig!'

'Ssh, Poppy.'

'Oh, Mum. Don't you see, now everyone will think he's *guilty*.'

'No, no,' protested Irena.

But Poppy knew she was right. With a feeling that she was growing up too fast, she thought, people *like* to think the worst, it actually gives them pleasure.

She remembered Jude's sly and excited expression. Even though Jude had said sorry, Poppy could never forgive her that.

'Well, it's done,' said her mum. 'Mr Hannigan was very understanding.'

They walked all the way home in silence and halfway back it began to rain, which was some kind of relief because they had to run.

When they'd dried off and Poppy was about to watch *Cheetah Kingdom*, her mum suddenly said timidly, 'I've fixed for us to go this Saturday, darling. That is, if you still want to.'

Poppy gulped. She didn't have to ask where they were going. 'OK,' she mumbled, as if it was nothing special, and went in to watch television.

Chapter Seven

Saturday. It was raining hard. Irena held an umbrella and Poppy pulled her hood up. They had to pass Will's house to get to the bus stop and they were hurrying along, heads down – prison visitors were only allowed in between certain times – when Poppy heard a shout.

She looked up and saw Will hanging out of his bedroom window with his thumb stuck high in the air.

'Good luck!' he yelled, before he was pulled back inside.

Irena looked up too. 'So Will knows where you're going.'

'Yes, Mum.' Poppy tried not to smile.

'What are you looking so cheerful about?' asked her mum.

'I'm looking forward to seeing Dad.'

'He's looking forward to it too.' Her mother had been in a state all morning, changing into one dress and then another, trying her hair up and then brushing it down.

Poppy had figured it didn't matter what you wore in prison, but when she put on her old jeans her mum had said, 'Don't you want to put on something nice for your dad?' So she changed into a pair of stripy cut-off trousers.

'That's better,' her mother said.

But now they'd be soaking wet when they arrived. Poppy's sandals were sodden.

'Run!' shouted Irena suddenly. There was a bus coming along as they approached the bus stop and the driver waited a second or two for them.

'I never knew I could run in these shoes before,' panted Irena, as they went up to the top of the bus.

Poppy looked at her two-inch high heels. Usually, her mum wore sensible flat slip-ons, 'so that I can give what-for to the pedals on the piano' (the 'what-for' sounding funny in her Polish accent).

It was only when they were settled that Poppy suddenly felt nervous.

'What will it be like, Mum?' she whispered.

'Well, first of all we go into the visitor's centre which is brand new and very nice.' Irena smiled in a thoroughly unconvincing way.

'Then what?' asked Poppy, adding, as her mum hesitated, 'Is the centre behind those great big high walls with the barbed wire on top?'

Irena looked at her sharply, 'What do you know about the walls?'

'It's like that in all the films.' Poppy felt herself blushing uncomfortably. She looked out of the window and wished the journey would never end.

But it did. She and her mum got off at the stop before the one she had got off with Will and walked along the other side of the road. A tube train running noisily to their left made Poppy jump.

They crossed the road and passed a row of grey, dismal-looking houses. 'You see, there're other children going there too,' said Irena in a trying-to-be-cheerful tone. Poppy put her head down.

When she next looked beyond her wet feet on the wet pavement, she saw some high railings and a trail of people going through them. They were not heading through the big gateway but to a building at the side of it.

'There!' said Irena, sweeping her arm like a tourist guide. 'Take at look at that grand entrance. It's probably been in half of those films you watch!' She gave a strangled gulp and stopped abruptly.

Poppy glanced up and saw two ornate towers on either side of an extremely large door. 'Yes' she agreed. She never ever wanted to watch another prison movie.

'The prison was first built in the 1880s,' mumbled Irena.

'How nice,' said Poppy, although she wanted to say, 'Stop trying to make things better, Mum.' As if it made any difference when this dreadful place was built! Unless, perhaps, it had ancient underground tunnels her dad could use as an escape route.

Thinking about this, Poppy followed her mother through a side gate and soon found herself in the visitor's centre. In fact it *was* rather nice, everything very clean and new. The receptionist even smiled at them.

While her mum was sorting things out, Poppy noticed the whole place was filled with leaflets, explaining all kinds of things, from visiting hours to special helpers called Samaritans. She decided to collect the lot and take them back to Will. Some of it had to be useful.

'Whyever have you got those?' asked Irena, returning at her most distracted.

'Something to read,' said Poppy.

'If you want to keep them, I have to put them in the locker with my handbag.'

'OK,' said Poppy. 'It says here that we can bring clothing in for Dad but not hooded jackets, hooded tracksuits, plain navy blue tracksuits, caps, hats, gloves and scarves and ties.'

When she next looked up, she noticed a boy about her age who was also collecting all the leaflets. He saw her staring and gave her a big wink. Poppy couldn't help smiling; he just had one of those faces. She watched him go back and sit with a woman, a younger girl and a baby. Again, he caught her eye and this time gave an expressive shrug as the baby let out a great howl.

They waited for nearly an hour as the room got fuller and fuller and Irena glanced at her watch more and more often. From her reading, Poppy discovered that you could post into the prison stationery, stamps, a religious medallion and a wedding ring but everything else had to go through the prison shop, library or an approved catalogue.

At last there was a sudden surge upwards as everyone round them stood up and headed for the door. Poppy found herself behind the boy, who was now holding the wailing baby.

'He's like a police siren,' said the boy.

'Ear-plugs?' suggested Poppy.

'We left them at home,' said the boy. He looked at Poppy over the head of the baby, who had the biggest brown eyes and the longest eyelashes she had ever seen. 'I'm called Angel. God's truth. What's yours?'

'Poppy.'

'Like in the fields.'

'And on Remembrance Sunday.'

By now they were moving out of the centre, through the impressive gate-house and into the prison itself. But Poppy was so busy with her new friend that she forgot to take note of the details which she'd promised Will to do – for escape purposes.

She couldn't miss the security, however. Two or three prison officers began to shout at them, 'Through the scanner and then over here for a pat-down.'

Poppy lost sight of Angel as she and her mum tried to do what they were told. She could hear the baby wailing from somewhere and wondered if he got patted down too.

When they'd finished the 'pat-down', which was horrid – a woman officer feeling all over her body – they were shepherded into a narrow space with glass doors on either side. One door shut behind them and, before the other opened, a group of them were crammed in together for several moments – which felt much longer. Poppy let out her breath as the other door opened.

'Call it the airlock, don't we,' said a kindly older woman who'd noticed Poppy's anxiety. 'Gives me claustrophobia every time.'

The real surprise came immediately afterwards, when two spaniel dogs came to greet them, sniffing round their legs.

'Poor things,' said Poppy, who liked animals, 'spending time in prison as if they were criminals.'

'They're just doing a job,' said the dog-handler, 'same as the rest of us.'

Poppy looked at the man who, like all the other prison staff, was wearing a white shirt with epaulettes, black trousers and a bunch of keys at his waist. It was odd to think he'd chosen to spend his time behind those terrible walls. His face seemed nice enough. Perhaps, if he knew Big Frank was innocent, he'd help Will and her to get him out.

'Do you *like* working in prison?' she asked, but he'd moved on with the dogs who were sniffing someone else, and didn't answer.

Now they were herded through more locked doors,

across a courtyard and into yet another waiting area. 'I've never waited so much in my life,' said Poppy to her mum, 'and why did those dogs sniff everybody? It's disgusting!'

Before Irena could answer, a cheerful voice pronounced, 'Drugs!'

'Hi,' said Poppy to Angel.

'Easy to tell you're fresh in,' said Angel. 'Looking for drugs, aren't they. Those dogs have noses like bloodhounds.' He paused. 'Guess they are bloodhounds.'

Poppy noticed that her mum was eyeing Angel in a not very friendly way.

'This is Angel,' she said, before Irena could move on. 'He's with that little girl and the baby.' She knew her mum would be suspicious of the way Angel looked, with his wild black curls and baggy, low-slung jeans.

'We're all angels,' said Angel. 'My sister's Seraphina and my baby bro's Gabriel. My mum is putting out for another called Raphael.' As Irena frowned, he added carelessly, 'My mum's very into God, on the angelic side.'

'My mum's Catholic,' contributed Poppy. 'So's my dad, really.'

As she said the word 'dad', she felt her face go bright red and her legs felt all wobbly.

'Inside, is he?'

'Yes,' mumbled Poppy, grabbing her mum's hand. How could she be chatting like this? Now she wanted to sit quietly with her mum and prepare to see Big Frank.

Angel seemed to get the message because he sloped off back to his own family, saying over his shoulder, 'See you.'

'Who is that boy?' whispered Irena.

'Just a boy.'

'He must be at least a couple of years older than you.'

Then they sat silently and Poppy could feel her mum's hand getting all sweaty, but she hung on all the same.

Soon after, there was another surge forward as in the visitor's centre, and Poppy realised that numbers were being called out.

'What's our number, Mum?'

'Z2717AB.'

'Z2717AB!' shouted a prison officer at the door.

Still holding hands tightly, Poppy and her mum walked quickly to the door.

Chapter Eight

At first Poppy couldn't see her dad. The room that they were led into was very big, very hot and already half-filled with people. They were formed into little groups, huddled together round tables as if expecting a storm to hit them. The tables and chairs were painted blue and bolted to the floor

Poppy noticed that her mum looked just as confused. Then she saw him.

'Dad!'

'Sshh.' Irena squeezed her hand nervously.

Poppy, who was about to run across the room, stopped abruptly. She was in prison. She must remember that. At each end of the room was a raised platform where two or three officers watched over the scene below them. Several more paced up and down the room, their keys jangling.

Poppy tried not to imagine what would happen if someone got out of line. Her legs felt wobbly again.

'Over there,' instructed an officer, looking at their number.

They walked over quietly and when they reached Big Frank he seemed subdued.

'Hi.' He stood up. He might be quiet, but he was as tall as ever. He kissed Irena and hugged Poppy. Usually when he did this, he lifted her off the ground so her whole body swung like a pendulum. This time he set her down quickly.

'Let's sit.' He spoke dully. No jokes.

What was Big Frank without jokes? Poppy sat down obediently. Her dad's face was much paler than normal and his hair seemed dimmer, too.

'You're not eating properly, are you?' said Irena reprovingly.

That was it, thought Poppy, he was a lot thinner.

'I'm fine,' said Frank. He patted his stomach and gave the pretence of a smile. 'I've been meaning to go on a diet for years.'

He turned to Poppy and addressed her for the first time. 'How are you, then? Having fun with Jude and all those nice friends of yours?'

Poppy stared at him. There was no way she could answer truthfully. 'I'm seeing more of Will.'

'Short for Wilhelmina?'

Poppy saw this was supposed to be a joke but couldn't bring herself to smile. 'He's a boy.'

'Aha! Into boys now!'

Poppy looked away, blushing. There was something embarrassing about her dad. She felt he was really very sad and wished he'd let it show instead of pretending.

'Will's very clever.' said Irena, trying to be helpful. 'Despite his health problems,' she added.

Poppy let her parents talk. She screwed her hands tightly together. She longed to be somewhere else, anywhere else. Over the other side of the room she caught sight of Angel. He seemed to be at a counter buying drinks.

'I'm thirsty,' said Poppy.

'Oh, yes. You too, Frank?' asked Irena, feeling in her pocket for the coins they'd been allowed to pick up again after going through the scanner.

Her dad had always been the one who paid for things. As Poppy stood up, she caught sight of his face; the expression on it reminded her of a small child who'd been seen doing something wrong. He looked ashamed.

But he's innocent! she thought. It's not his fault he's in this weird place.

'Hiya.' Angel was still standing by the canteen. 'Enjoying being a film star, are you?' He raised his eyes and, following his gaze, Poppy saw that there were cameras directed at every table.

'It's horrible here, isn't it!' Suddenly overcome by everything, Poppy only just managed to stop herself bursting into tears.

'You get used to it. Some of the kids even enjoy it.' He pointed to where some younger children were playing with toys in a special area. He turned back to the counter. 'Want me to order for you?'

'Coffee, tea and diet coke,' said Poppy. She was still thinking about her dad. 'But he's *innocent*!'

'Cheers.' Angel used a voice as if he was patting a puppy on the head. Then he ordered the drinks.

'What do you mean?' asked Poppy suspiciously.

'All our dads are innocent, aren't they. My dad's been in and out four times since I can remember and he's always innocent, isn't he.'

There was no question mark at the end of the sentence. Poppy glanced back at her dad, now huddled with her mum against the storm like all the others. She supposed all the turned backs were because they were avoiding the cameras. 'But my dad *is* innocent!'

"Course he is, like I said before.' Angel picked up his drinks. 'Better go.'

Poppy was sure he didn't believe her, and thought of one way of showing him she was serious. 'I'm going to help my dad escape from here. That's how much I know he's innocent!'

Angel stopped and, for a moment, Poppy suspected he was going to laugh. Instead he asked softly, 'How you planning on that?'

'Will and I have done a recce already. We. . .'

'Not here.' Angel interrupted. He nodded at the prison officers all around. 'I'll catch you at school one day.'

'School?' Poppy gawped. 'We're not at the same school, are we?'

'St Augustus of the Holy Angels. My mum rates that school.'

'But I've never seen you.'

'I'm in the top year. Don't mix, do we.'

With that, Angel left and Poppy, perilously balancing her two cups and a can, headed across the room. On her way she passed a couple who were having a row. They had been whispering, but suddenly the man shouted a swear word at the top of his voice. Immediately, two prison officers closed in.

65

Immediately the room felt full of danger.

Poppy hurried back to her mum and dad.

'Thanks.' They hardly looked up from their conversation. Poppy thought her mum had been crying.

'Did I say tea?' Irena pushed the cup away.

'Sorry,' said Poppy. How could anything be right in a place like this? The man who had shouted was being hustled forcibly out of the room. He was tall with an ugly big paunch. His girlfriend was crying noisily. A woman nearby tried to console her but she pushed her away roughly.

'I'll tell you what,' Irena stood up, 'I'll go. You talk to your dad for a bit.'

Big Frank said nothing. so Poppy sat down opposite him, feeling awkward. Now was the time to mention the Great Escape. But he wasn't even looking at her. Maybe she'd lead in gradually.

'Is your room – er – cell near here?'

Frank seemed puzzled by the question. 'Sorry, Pops, what did you say?'

'I wondered where your cell was?'

'Whether it has a nice view, you mean.' His smile was a bit ironic, but friendly too.

'I mean, is it far from here?'

This time Frank gave a genuine laugh. 'That's a question I didn't expect. Next time you visit, I'll count how many doors the guard has to unlock and lock again to get me here. At least a dozen, I'd say.'

'But do you live in the East, West, South or North block?' This was a question Will had prepared.

'Well, now.' Frank looked round. 'Which way are we facing, would you say? It seems to me we'd need a compass to work that one out.' He paused and grinned at Poppy, 'You're not trying to spring me, are you?'

Blushing, Poppy was about to answer, 'Actually, yes,' when her mother came back.

Big Frank winked, and Poppy decided he knew her answer anyway. The only person who had winked like her dad was Angel. Strange, that. She tried to decide if Will and Angel would get on and thought, probably not.

'They'll turn us out soon,' said Irena. 'Anything you want to tell your dad, Poppy?'

Poppy thought she'd already told him the most important thing. 'What's your cell like?' she asked.

'Oh, Poppy,' protested Irena.

'You like that word "cell", don't you, darling?' It was the first time Frank had used the word 'darling', and it made Poppy feel tearful all over again.

'I just want to know what it's like,' she persevered.

'The bad bits or the good bits?'

'Oh, Frank,' Irena protested to her husband.

'I'll tell you.' Frank leant forward. 'The good bits: in-cell television.'

'That's great!' exclaimed Poppy.

'The bad bits:' went on Frank. 'My cell-mate's taste in TV programmes, his smelly feet and his whiny voice. Then there's in-cell sanitation, i.e. a toilet beside your bed, a hole in the door so you can be watched, the door itself, which is mostly locked and, worst of all,' he took Irena's hand on one side and Poppy's hand on the other, 'not being with my darlings.'

These bitter words completely silenced Irena and Poppy. They stared at Big Frank miserably.

'Time! Time's up, ladies and gentlemen!' The prison officers had come off their platforms and were advancing in a meaningful, heavy-footed way.

The woman whose man had been taken away began arguing loudly with a guard. She kept yelling, 'I've come all the way from Sheffield.' Everywhere there was hugging and kissing – and crying too. Poppy could distinctly hear Gabriel's wails. She could have wailed herself as Big Frank stood up, muttering, 'Like pub closing time, except we've missed out on the booze.'

Poppy wanted to kiss him once and then run away, but there were queues of people trying to get out and, anyway, her mum was still clinging to her dad.

'Sshh, darling,' said Big Frank, putting her gently aside. He was the one who walked away, with all the other men, heads down, not talking to each other.

This was the very worst moment, thought Poppy, saying goodbye, and leaving her dad to his cell behind the walls with the barbed wire, the stony-faced officers and the beastly sniffer dogs. It made her even more determined to get him out.

But Will would have been disappointed in her as they left the room and made their way back to the prison entrance. Poppy was too upset to notice how many doors were unlocked and locked or which way they were heading.

It was only when they were outside the prison and crossing the courtyard to the visitors' centre, that Poppy glanced backwards.

'I wonder where Dad is now?' She said to her mum.

'Behind the walls,' answered Irena, sadly.

She seemed to be about to say something else, before stopping herself.

Then they were back in the crowds at the visitors' centre and queuing for their things from the locker. Everyone round them wore the same dazed look.

'Do you really want all these leaflets?' asked Poppy's mum.

'Yes. I do.' At least she'd have something to show Will.

As they turned to go, Angel caught up with her. He was again holding Gabriel, now gurgling with happiness as if he'd never been called a police siren.

'He's like all of us,' said Angel laconically, 'prefers out to in.'

'But our dads are still in.' Poppy felt her voice wavering.

'So they are.' Angel hurried to catch up with his mum and his sister, then called back over his shoulder, 'Got to sort out that, haven't we?'

'Who *is* that boy?' said Irena distractedly.

'No one,' answered Poppy. But actually, he was *someone* who she wanted to see again.

They stood on the pavement outside the prison gates. Poppy took huge gulps of fresh air, free air. It was extraordinary how quickly the crowds had disappeared, and now they seemed to be on an ordinary London street. A bus passed one way; beyond the road a tube passed the other way. A few pedestrians walked casually by.

It had stopped raining and turned into a nice sunny Saturday afternoon. No one seemed in much of a hurry.

'It's stopped raining,' said Irena.

Poppy turned round to look at the prison behind her. 'It's as if it's invisible, isn't it? No one takes any notice of it, as if it isn't there.'

'They've got better things to think about,' said her mum without turning her head.

'All those men inside their cells, locked up, just a few yards away,' began Poppy, trying to work out what seemed so odd, 'and people going about as if they didn't exist.'

'It's no different from a hospital, is it?' Irena began to walk towards the bus stop.

'But people go inside hospitals,' said Poppy. 'They don't know about prisons.'

'Who wants to know about prisons?' said her mum. She was walking more quickly now.

'But there are people inside. Dads.'

'Please, Poppy!' Irena put her hand to her head.

'I know you're right. It's not fair on you, but please can you be quiet now. I've got a splitting headache and I've three pupils this afternoon.'

Poppy felt sorry for her mum so she shut up, even though she hadn't managed to explain what she meant. It wasn't about things being unfair on her. It was something to do with prison being secret, as if it wasn't there at all.

Chapter Nine

Will's mum opened their front door.

'He's not so great this afternoon,' she said. She was a brisk sort of woman, always busy. Poppy supposed that's why she became a GP. She ushered Poppy in. 'Will's in bed, but you might cheer him up.'

Poppy walked up the stairs slowly. Will had enjoyed doing those clever pictures of her dad waving from the turrets. Probably he wasn't serious about the escape plan. Going inside the huge walls had made the task of getting her dad out seem harder, not easier.

'Hi.'

'Hi.' Will looked about six years old, propped up in his bed. He'd been reading, Poppy saw, on a Kindle.

'I didn't know you had one of those.' Poppy, feeling rather jealous, sat on the end of his bed.

'When my eyes are tired, I can make the print bigger. It doesn't weigh much, either. I prefer real books, though. Or my Warhammer figures.' He waved to a table completely covered with fierce little figures. 'I like Ogre Kingdoms Ironguts best,' he added.

There was a pause. Shyly, Poppy waited for him to ask about her visit.

'Sorry,' he said eventually. 'When I feel like this, I don't have much energy. How was your dad?'

'Bad,' said Poppy. She didn't really want to talk about her dad. That wasn't Will's business. His job was to help get Big Frank out. But at the moment, he didn't look able to do more than press the buttons on his Kindle, which is what he was doing. Not the perfect co-conspirator!

For a moment Poppy pictured Angel, with all his energy and confidence. Now, *he* was the right kind of gang member.

Reluctantly she opened a bag she'd brought with her and emptied out the papers and leaflets she'd brought from the prison. 'Here's some useful info,' she said, sounding more optimistic than she felt.

Will picked up a coloured brochure. 'My visit', he read. He flipped through the pages. 'It looks like something at playschool. Things to colour.'

'Some of the kids were really young.' said Poppy. 'Even babies.'

'In prison?' exclaimed Will.

'Suppose they didn't know where they were.'

'Suppose not.' Will read out, '*If you would like to send money to your relative or friend in Grisewood Slops Prison, you need to send them a postal order..*' He looked up. 'I thought postal orders had gone out with the dinosaurs.'

'Obviously not in prisons,' said Poppy.

Will continued reading, '*The postal order must be made payable to 'The Governor'. You must write the name and prison number of the inmate on the back of the postal order.*' Will looked up again, 'Does he have a number, then, your dad?'

'Z2717AB. It's humiliating, isn't it – being known by a number.'

'You could pretend he's entered a marathon,' suggested Will.

'There'd have to be an awful lot of runners.'

Will picked up another leaflet. '*We deliver newspapers and magazines to HMP Grisewood Slops*' – that's a bit civilised.'

'He won't be in long enough to order newspapers!' said Poppy. She was losing her patience. 'We *are* going to get him out, aren't we?'

Will lay back in his bed. 'Did you get an idea

which part of the prison your dad's in?'

He asked so half-heartedly that it hardly seemed worth answering. Not that Poppy had an answer. 'There were sniffer dogs,' she said.

'What make of dogs?'

'Spaniels.'

'I'd pictured ferocious Alsatians.'

'Maybe Spaniels have sharper noses,' said Poppy. It was as if they were having a chat about things that didn't really matter – when it was her dad's life at stake.

'Maybe they have Alsatians patrolling the walls,' suggested Will.

Poppy didn't answer. Will was ill. Of course he wasn't getting excited about things like scaling walls and evading armed guards. He preferred them lined up on a table like his Warhammer figures.

'Poppy! You should come down now!' It was Will's mum calling from downstairs.

'Bye,' said Poppy. 'See you at school.'

'Yes. Here, take these.'

Poppy stuffed the leaflets back into her bag, thinking Will wasn't even interested enough to want to study them carefully.

'Time's up,' called his mum, reminding Poppy

uncomfortably of the prison officer in the visiting room. She realised that she now knew about something that absolutely nobody else knew about in school.

Then she remembered Angel.

Monday morning wasn't a good time any more. Miss Bavani's face writhed in and out like a mask as she spoke, and Poppy didn't hear a word she said. For several minutes she had the same face as one of the prison officers.

At break, even though it was still spitting with rain, Poppy went straight out to the playground, to a corner behind a wall where children up to no good usually gathered. Will was not in school, presumably still sick, and there was no one else she felt like talking to.

'Hiya!' Angel appeared from nowhere.

'How did you get here?' Poppy moved back nervously.

'Angelic, aren't I. Supernatural, like I go through walls like you go through air.'

Poppy stared. She couldn't think what to say. He was so unlike her friends – but then she reminded herself, she had no friends.

'I know what you're thinking,' Angel carried on perkily, 'Pity I can't pass on my gift to my dad, stuck behind bars.'

Unconsciously, Poppy looked over her shoulder. Were they going to talk about prison openly, here in the playground, even if they were a bit hidden?

'Funny, I've never seen you at school before.'

'We run in a different crowd, don't we. And I'm older. I saw the way your mum looked at me.'

'My mum's all right,' said Poppy. 'She's just unhappy.'

'Takes mums that way. At least, at first.' Angel came closer. 'So what's this plan you and your friend – "Won't", isn't it?'

'Will,' said Poppy.

'Will you, won't you.' Angel laughed at his own joke. 'So how do you plan getting your innocent dad out of the nick?'

Poppy didn't like Angel's mocking tone, but just at the moment he was the only one showing any interest. 'Will's ill,' she said.

'So you're on hold?'

'Sort of.' Poppy tried to sound more positive. 'We've drawn up a plan of the outside of the p—', she hesitated at the word, 'nick, and now I'm

78

trying to work out how it fits with the inside.'

'Your dad knows what you're up to, does he?'

'Oh, yes,' replied Poppy airily, although she suspected her dad hadn't taken in what she'd told him.

'Thing is. . .' – much to Poppy's surprise, Angel took out an iPad from a bag he was carrying – 'not many escape from Grisewood Slops. Not these days. Other prisons, yes.' He started started running his finger over the screen. 'But they're mostly the open sort where people are working outside anyway, and just have to walk away – well, catch a bus. You know.'

'Will was talking about Colditz,' said Poppy, trying to keep her end up.

'That's in World War II. There's Alcatraz, too. An island in the U.S. Three men made a boat out of mackintoshes and were never seen again. Drowned, probably.'

'Oh,' said Poppy.

'Don't get me wrong, I'm not trying to put you off. You should get your dad out because he's innocent and not many can say that and it's true. . .'

'It *is* true,' interrupted Poppy.

'I'm just saying, it's not easy. We'll have to think.'

Poppy clocked the 'we'.

'It's a bit of a challenge, that's what I'm saying. What's your dad charged with?'

'I don't know.' Noticing Angel's surprise, Poppy added, 'My mum didn't tell me.'

'No. . . It makes no difference, suppose, if he's innocent. Tell you what, I've got to go.'

Poppy heard the bell ring for classes, but Angel was slipping backwards behind the building. 'Aren't you coming into school?'

'Later. I'll check out what wing your dad's on. Let you know. See ya.' Then he was gone.

Poppy walked slowly back across the empty playground. She thought of Angel's iPad – forbidden in school – and his disappearance when the bell rang. It was obvious that he played by his own rules, and not just because he was older. Her mum was right to be suspicious. But who else was around to help her?

At lunchtime, Poppy was prepared to sit on her own but, as she picked up her food, Jude approached.

'Hi.' Jude hovered. Amber came up on Poppy's other side. She knew they wanted her to sit with them. They were sorry for her and this was a kind of apology. Poppy hesitated. Then Jude took her arm with her free hand.

It was strange sitting with her old friends. It all seemed just as it used to be.

'Did you see,' giggled Jude, 'Mr Hannigan's new drain-pipe trousers?'

'Not so much drain-pipe as pipe-cleaner,' said Amber.

The trouble was that they were exactly the same as they'd always been, fun and friendly – and she was completely different. How could she joke about the headmaster's silly trousers when her dad was locked up in a cell? In PRISON? In a way, even though she'd actually been there, she still couldn't believe it was true. When she'd gone to the prison, it had been like Alice going down the hole and finding a whole new world which only she knew about. Of course, that wasn't quite true; her mum knew about it, Angel knew about it. But even Will only knew about it in theory.

Her mum and Angel were the only people who really understood. They were the only people she wanted to be with. Maybe Will too, because of the Great Escape Plan.

'You're quiet,' said Jude.

'Sorry,' said Poppy. 'I'm not really hungry. I'll see you later.'

She stood up and as she did, saw the expression on Jude's face change. 'Going to see that boy, are you?'

At first Poppy assumed she meant Will, but Will wasn't in school, so then she realised someone had seen her with Angel.

'I'm not going to see anyone,' she said, before adding crossly, 'and if I was, it would be none of your business!'

So that was the end of trying to be friends with Jude again. She was a nosey, nasty person, thought Poppy, and went to lock herself in the toilet, which seemed to be the only place where she could be alone and not spied on.

Chapter Ten

After school, Poppy called in on Will. He was downstairs and seemed much livelier. He was looking at his mum's laptop. He was on his own, although he said a neighbour was keeping an eye on him.

'Guess what I can see!' he said with a triumphant air.

'What?' Poppy dumped her bag on the floor.

'Her Majesty's Prison Grisewood Slops. Just googled it. All kinds of useful info.'

Poppy peered over his shoulder. 'Angel was looking up things on his iPad.'

'Who's Angel?' asked Will suspiciously.

'Boy I met in the prison,' Poppy slumped down on the sofa. 'Didn't I tell you.'

'No.' Will sounded offended.

'Well, you weren't well, were you.'

'No.' repeated Will, sounding even more offended.

'He's going to help us,' said Poppy. 'His dad's been

83

in and out of the nick lots of times so he's been visiting since he was a little kid.' '

'What's the nick?'

'Prison, isn't it? Angel knows all kinds of things.'

'What kind of things?' Will still sounded huffy.

'He's going to find out which wing Big Frank's on.'

'It says about wings here.' Will read off the screen, 'Grisewood Slops is a Category B prison for adult males, sentenced or on remand from the local courts. The prison has five main wings.'

'What *is* a wing?' Poppy hadn't dared ask Angel in case he thought she was stupid.

'Like a corridor with cells off it, I guess. There's A, B, C, D and E plus something called a super-enhanced wing where especially trustworthy prisoners live. Then there's another wing where,' he began to read again, stumbling a bit over the words, 'prisoners live who require a substance misuse stabilisation regime.'

'Drugs,' said Poppy. 'That's what the dogs are sniffing for. Angel told me.'

At the mention of his name, Will looked suspicious all over again. 'You know, you shouldn't tell people about our escape plan. Word might get out.'

'Angel isn't "people". We weren't getting very far on our own, anyway. With you ill.'

'Actually, I've got a plan for tomorrow. My mum is out on late call so we can borrow her camera, take some photos of the prison, print them off on our computer, then delete everything before she's back.'

'Brilliant!'

Poppy was wondering what excuse she could think up to go home late after school when Will, who was back to fiddling with the laptop, called out 'Hey! Just look at this. *Escape from HMP Grisewood Slops, out through a window, over the wall and into hiding!*'

'However did he do that? Angel said no one gets out.'

'Hang on. Let me read.'

Poppy waited impatiently. She thought, so it *has* been done. It *can* be done!

'Quite simple,' said Will. 'He cut out a pane from a window at the end of his corridor, removed the bar and squeezed through while everyone else was watching a film. Then he went to the perimeter wall where friends from outside had thrown up a ladder, and climbed over. That was it.'

'It sounds so easy.' Poppy thought of the stony-faced guards and the sniffer dogs and the barbed wire. 'There are two sets of walls,' she said, 'and barbed wire.'

Will looked again. 'Bad news.'

'What?'

'That prisoner escaped in the 1960s.'

'Nearly half a century ago! My dad wasn't even born then. I expect everything's changed since.'

'They've still got to have windows,' said Will, but he sounded deflated.

'I think your photograph idea is a good one,' said Poppy to cheer him up. His head was still bent over the laptop.

'2005.' He was reading again. 'That's more like it. *Minister asks questions as prisoner walks to freedom.*'

'Whatever do you mean? No one can walk over two walls.'

'Hold on. *Yesterday afternoon, a prisoner from HMP Grisewood Slops was escorted to an outside hospital for an emergency check. He never returned to prison and remains at large.*'

'Has he swollen up or something?'

Will laughed. 'It just means, he's out in the larger world. Free, in other words.' He looked up. 'How did your dad seem? Feeling OK?'

'He was pale and thin,' said Poppy. 'Still, not thin enough to get through a window.'

'No,' Will seemed doubtful. 'It's clever, though,

isn't it. Just to walk out. No problem. The one who got out of the window broke his ankle getting over the wall. The hospital idea seems much better.'

'Yeah. I'll keep thinking.'

*

Walking home, Poppy tried to imagine what Big Frank was doing at that moment. He'd said he had TV, so perhaps he was watching *Dr Who*. They'd always liked watching it together while her mum played the piano upstairs.

'Hi, Mum!' Poppy opened her front door, shouted and dumped her bag. 'It's me,' she called again. But she got no answer.

Usually her mum wanted a hug when she got in. Poppy opened the kitchen door and there she was, on the phone. She flapped her hands at Poppy, either telling her to stay or go; Poppy didn't know which – so she stayed.

After a few moments of listening, Irena mouthed to Poppy, 'It's your dad.'

Poppy sat down. It seemed weird that her dad's voice could come into the kitchen when he was locked away. But that was silly, when phones went everywhere now. Probably you could get a call even if you were on a desert island in the middle of a faraway ocean.

'Here. Quick, Poppy.' Her mum waved her over. 'He's nearly out of money.'

'Hi, Dad. How are you?'

'Not so good today, Popsicles. My tummy's had enough of being fed on two pounds a day.'

'What do you mean?' Poppy's heart gave a lurch. Had Will's talk about her dad escaping if he was ill actually made him sick?

'Stomach cramps. Not to worry. I've bent your mother's ear till it's nearly off. Good day?'

But just as Poppy was thinking what to answer, the phone went dead.

Seeing her surprised expression, Irena took the phone back.

'Dad says he's got stomach cramps.' The way Poppy said it, it sounded as if she was accusing her mum, but Irena didn't seem to notice.

'Never had a day's illness, your dad. A great big healthy fellow. That's what a couple of weeks in prison does to you.'

Poppy thought to herself, that's why we've got to get him out. To her mum, she said, 'Will he have to go to hospital?'

'Oh, I don't think it's that bad.' Irena turned away. 'What do you like for tea?'

Poppy thought, her mum shouldn't pretend everything was normal. How could she eat tea when Big Frank was in prison with stomach cramps? However, she answered, 'Baked beans,' because it was easy.

If Big Frank did go to hospital, it just might be the best thing ever.

Chapter Eleven

'Hiya!'

Angel appeared in that sudden way of his. It was school break-time.

'Hi.'

'You're *innocent* dad's on A wing,' Angel said right away. Poppy wished he wouldn't sound as if he was making a joke about her dad's innocence. 'Same wing as my dad,' Angel added. 'Which might be useful.'

'Oh, yes.' Over Angel's shoulder, Poppy noticed Will approaching. They couldn't have been more different – both from each other and everyone else – Angel with his mass of black hair, low-slung trousers and confident slouch, and Will so thin and pale and intense.

'My dad's out soon, as it happens,' Angel said.

'Out,' repeated Poppy, stupidly. 'Because he's innocent?'

Angel stared at her as. 'Because he's done his time. Not that I'll see much of him. He'll be up to his usual tricks.'

Poppy was struggling with the idea that there were men around who had been in prison. Men who were not innocent – in other words, guilty!

'You mean, he could pick you up from school.'

'Some chance.'

'But he could.'

'Could if he would. Wouldn't if he could.' Angel turned the line into a song and tapped his feet.

Poppy saw Will hesitate, as if trying to decide whether to turn back.

'Here's my friend Will,' she said.

Angel turned. 'Hiya.'

'Hi.' Will shuffled around.

'This is Angel,' said Poppy nervously.

'I guessed,' said Will.

And Angel laughed. Somehow the laugh broke the tension and the boys gave each other high-fives, although, as usual, Will wasn't much good at it.

'We're going to photograph Grisewood Slops after school. Want to come?'

'Maybe.'

The bell rang for the end of break and Angel sloped off.

'Do you think he'll come?' asked Will, as they went to the classroom.

'Don't know.' Poppy wasn't sure she understood anything much about Angel.

Catching the bus to the prison was becoming quite a habit, Poppy thought. Will said he'd rather not climb upstairs, so they sat together behind the driver.

'I spoke to Big Frank yesterday,' said Poppy. For some reason she still hadn't told Will about her dad being ill. She suspected Will would say, 'That's terrific. Now we've got a real chance of getting him out. . .' and it didn't seem right to be pleased if her dad was ill.

'I've got a camera,' said Will.

'I suppose we could have taken photos on our mobiles.'

'Not such good quality.' Will sounded cross and Poppy suspected he still wasn't feeling well.

As they got off the bus there was a sudden noise above their heads. Looking up, Poppy saw Jude and Amber and several other girls banging on the window at the top of the bus and shouting her name.

Blushing scarlet, she waved briefly and followed Will, who'd already started walking towards the prison. The bus started, and as it overtook her, she caught a glimpse of the girls still waving and banging.

What must they think? That she was visiting her dad with Will? What would they be imagining? It made her squirm with embarrassment. Thank goodness Angel hadn't appeared!

Just then, there was a squeal of brakes and protesting tyres.

'Hey!' Angel was at the kerbside astride a magnificent bike, the sun glinting off its handlebars. He was wearing a lime-green T-shirt which also seemed to glint and gleam.

'That's quite a bike,' said Poppy.

'Present from my dad.'

Poppy thought that his dad must be doing quite well, even if he was in prison. By now, Will had come back to join them.

'Don't want to draw attention to ourselves, do we?' He looked disapprovingly at Angel.

Angel smiled. 'Just had a bit of news from inside.' He nodded in the direction of the prison, 'Your dad's not too well. They might take him to the hospital.'

'Poppy!' Will turned on her reproachfully. 'Did you know? And not tell me?'

Poppy's hot blushes (her first lot of blushes had only just subsided) gave him the answer.

'Best chance of escape,' continued Angel.

'That's just what I was telling her last night!' interrupted Will.

Angel glanced at him before continuing, 'Although the hospital's just down the road.'

'You mean, he'd walk?' asked Poppy.

'No chance. Into the sweat box, even for a couple of metres.'

'What's the sweat box?' asked Poppy.

'Van for transporting prisoners,' said Angel. 'Six or more of them squeezed into little cages. No ventilation. Sweat boxes.'

I suppose my poor dad travelled in the sweat box to the prison, thought Poppy, but she didn't say anything because she didn't want to interrupt the planning.

'We've got to get to the screws,' continued Angel

'Bribe the prison officers, you mean?' said Will.

'That's it. Depends who they are, of course. My dad might be able to fix that.'

Will and Poppy looked at each other. When they made plans, it all seemed a bit fantastical, as if it came out of a film, but Angel's ideas sounded as if they really might happen.

'Another thing.' Angel was rolling his wheels backwards and forwards. His bicycle seemed like a powerful horse pawing the ground, impatient to be off.

'No point in taking those pix.' He extracted a piece of folded paper from his pocket which, because his jeans were so low-slung, nearly reached his knees. 'Internet,' he said, as Poppy took the paper and opened it.

Will looked over her shoulder. 'I missed that,' he muttered. The photograph showed a good aerial view of the prison – far more useful than anything they could get.

'Blueprint for escape,' said Angel, 'See you.' And he was on his bike and away.

'Seems to be allowed to do anything he wants,' said Will grumpily.

'I suppose if your dad's. . .' began Poppy. She had been going to say 'If your dad's in prison, there's more freedom,' until she remembered that her dad was in prison and it didn't give her more freedom.

'If we're not going to take the photographs, I'd better go home,' she said instead.

'I might as well snap a few since we're here,' said Will, and Poppy thought that he didn't want to hand everything over to Angel. She thrust the internet map more firmly into her pocket. It seemed odd that anyone could print it off the internet, but all the better.

They walked on towards the front of the prison. Although they were on the other side of the road with the tube train running noisily behind them, Poppy felt exposed. What would people think of two children standing staring at the prison gates?

'If I get out my camera, they might think we're spying,' said Will.

'I was thinking just the same. What if the screws' – Angel's name for prison officers – 'look out and see us?'

'They might arrest us.'

We're not exactly a threat, are we?' Poppy tried to sound bold. 'I mean, we've only got a camera – not knives.'

'Or guns.'

'Of course we haven't got guns. All we've got is your mum's camera.'

Will frowned. He seemed unwilling to give up the sense of danger. Poppy supposed that if you were ill so much, you longed for excitement. The point was, it wasn't his dad in prison. *He* hadn't been inside. So it probably wasn't completely real for him. Just good fun. Like his Ogre Kingdoms Ironlungs.

'We *are* a threat because we're planning a Great Escape!' said Will firmly.

'Why don't you take the photographs, then?'

'OK. OK.'

In the end, Poppy stood half in front of Will while he lined up his photograph and then stood aside at the last minute. As Will was taking his third photo and Poppy was saying, 'That's it, then,' they both got a sudden shock as the massive red prison door between the two towers opened and out drove a white van at speed. It turned right and passed on their side of the road so that they could see the darkened windows and the two uniformed drivers.

'A sweat box,' breathed Will, taking a quick photo.

But Poppy turned away. It made her feel sick that her dad might be inside.

'It's not going in the direction of the hospital,' said Will, as if reading her thoughts.

On the way back, Poppy was very quiet. The bus was crammed full so that they had to stand. Even so, Will kept trying to talk, in a kind of coded way so that she hadn't any idea what he was saying – except that it was something to do with the escape, which he referred to as 'ESCP'.

When they parted, he was still talking, promising a new drawing based on the print-out of the photographs.

'That's a good idea,' said Poppy, which was a lie because the more she thought about the prison, the less likely it seemed they'd ever get her dad out that way. It was the hospital plan or nothing.

Wearily, she put her key in her front door.

'Where were you? Where've you gone?' When Irena was upset, her English had a way of letting her down. Now she was very upset. 'Will's Mama came home early and no Will. No Poppy!'

'Oh, Mum.' Poppy tried to sound casual. 'We went for a walk, that's all.'

'Walk! You walk!' Irena waved her hands in the air. 'And you not tell me! Your mama. You turn off your phone.'

'We went for a walk, Mum. It's not like we're in prison. If we want. . .' Poppy stopped. How had prison popped out like that!

'Oh, my Poppy!' Now her mum was in tears.

By tea-time, everything was back to normal and Poppy was even considering doing her homework, when her mum suddenly said, 'I forget' – perhaps her English wasn't quite back to normal – 'Jude rang. She said your mobile was off, which of course I also know.'

'What did she say?' Instantly Poppy was on her guard. Had Jude told her mum where she'd seen her?

'Nothing. She said nothing.'

Chapter Twelve

'What were you doing outside that prison yesterday?'

Poppy had no time to think what to say to Jude, because she caught up with her on the way to school.

'What do you think I was doing?'

'Did you go inside?

'I have been.' By now they were walking side by side with Jude's brothers ahead and Irena behind, talking on her mobile. It was quite like old times.

'Was it terrifying?' Jude's eyes were wide.

'Oh, yes,' said Poppy carelessly. As if she'd tell Jude the truth of it – the endless waiting, queuing, being searched, seeing her dad like a sad stranger. All the people so upset around her. 'There are sniffer dogs,' she added.

'Alsatians,' breathed Jude.

'Looking for drugs,' said Poppy, avoiding telling her that the dogs were Spaniels.

'And did you see lots of dangerous men? Murderers? Rapists? Kidnappers?'

'They don't wear labels round their necks, saying "Burglar" or "Murderer",' Poppy said tartly. 'For all I know, they might be innocent, like my dad.'

'You mean, they're all in it together?'

But Poppy was tired of the game. She thought, Jude only wants details so she can tell Amber and the others.

'If your dad's innocent, he'll be let out,' said Jude.

'Can't be soon enough.' Poppy began to walk faster.

'My mum says he hasn't been tried yet.' Jude caught her up. 'She'd heard it was coming up soon. In court, she told me.'

Poppy said nothing because she was so shocked. Her mum hadn't told her that.

Jude took hold of her arm, 'Want to meet after school?'

'Perhaps.' Poppy knew Jude was not just out to get the gossip, that she really meant to be kind, but she was too confused to act on it. 'I've got to catch up with some work.'

'You can't miss *Dr Who*.'

Poppy thought that even *Dr Who* didn't seem very important any more. 'Perhaps,' she said again.

The rest of the day seemed too long. Will was off sick again, so Poppy didn't even have him to talk to. At lunch break, her old friends were all gathered in a corner talking about the new Sarah Jane Adventures. She could hear their excited voices and was tempted to join them. Instead she sat on a wall in the sun and tried to read a book about outer space. But she didn't have the energy for that, either. Sadness was very tiring. No wonder her mum came back from her piano lessons far too exhausted to talk to her about anything important. Like her dad going to court.

'Want the good news or the bad news?' Angel had done his usual here-I-am-out-of-the-blue trick.

'Good, please,' said Poppy.

'Your dad's in the pink of health.'

'What's the bad?'

'That's the bad news too. No chance of escaping.'

'Oh.'

'Reading, are you?' Angel pointed at her book.

'Sort of.'

'I've never got on with books. Too fake. If I was a writer, I'd put down what was happening in real life, on the streets, in people's homes. Not magic stuff.'

'But you *must* like Harry Potter books.'

'Kids' stuff.' Angel shrugged.

'But you *are* a kid.'

'The movies are all right. But you just sit there, don't you. Just sit and let it wash over you. Not like having to read all that rubbish.'

Poppy wondered, but obviously couldn't ask, just how good Angel's reading was. As far as she could make out, he didn't spend much time in school. 'I like reading in bed before I go to sleep,' she said.

'Too much noise at my place. Gabriel's usually stuffed in with me, for starters. Our flat's like Piccadilly Circus. Everyone up all hours.'

Poppy thought this sounded fun. 'There's only my mum and me at home. It's very quiet.' She paused. 'Of course, it's different when my dad's there.'

Angel looked at his feet. He was wearing large silver blue and white trainers. They must have been very expensive.

'I spoke to my dad last night.' He hesitated.

'Does your dad call every night?'

'Day too. Got a mobile, hasn't he.'

'I didn't know mobiles were allowed in the nick!'

Angel laughed. 'Not allowed. Off regulations. Doesn't mean my dad hasn't got one.'

'I see,' said Poppy, thinking it was no wonder Angel broke school rules with a dad like that.

'My dad said last night,' Angel began again, 'that your dad's in court soon.'

'I know,' said Poppy quickly.

'Yeah.' Angel looked relieved. 'You know what he's pleading, then?'

'What's "pleading"?'

'Pleading?' Angel looked confused, as if he wasn't used to explaining words. 'Like saying where he stands. Giving his p.o.v.'

'So what point of view's that?' said Poppy, who still didn't understand.

'He's pleading guilty, isn't he. Done a plea bargain, my dad said, turned in one or two others. That kind of thing.'

'Guilty,' repeated Poppy, a horrible feeling starting in her stomach.

Angel stopped and looked at her. 'He won't get so long inside, then.'

'But he's innocent!' cried out Poppy.

'I didn't say he wasn't innocent, did I? I said he's pleading guilty. Gets him a shorter sentence, doesn't it.'

Poppy felt as if her head was bursting. 'But if he's

innocent, he shouldn't get any sentence at all.'

'That's the law for you.' Poppy noticed that Angel's eyes didn't meet hers and his big silver-blue trainers were moving about as if they wanted to carry away their owner.

'You don't believe he's innocent, do you?' she said unhappily.

'All dads are innocent. Didn't I say that first time we met?' Poppy could see his relief when the bell went.

'I suppose you're off somewhere exciting,' she said bitterly.

'Classroom,' Angel grinned. 'Last chance saloon. My dad'll murder me if I get excluded. And he's out next week.'

That evening Irena spent hours playing passionate tunes on the piano. When Poppy looked in – after all, it was her bedroom – tears were pouring down her mum's face and dripping on the keys. 'It is Chopin,' she cried, without stopping playing. 'He has the heart and emotions of a Polish genius!'

Poppy shut the door. She tried to remember why

the piano couldn't be in the downstairs living room. Something to do with her dad and his work and the TV, she thought. But now he wasn't here, it was silly.

Then she thought, he *will* be here soon. Going to the telephone, she rang Will's number.

'Hi, Will.'

'Hi, Poppy. What news?' He sounded eager but his voice was weak.

Poppy considered what to tell him. Instead, she asked, 'What happened to the prison pictures?'

'My mum took the camera. She deleted everything without looking because she said she respected my privacy. They weren't much good, anyway.'

'That figures.'

'So, now it's Hospital Escape Plan.'

Poppy knew she should tell him her dad was well again but didn't want to disappoint him.

'Sure, Plan B.'

'Big Frank and me might meet there.' said Will.

'Whatever do you mean?'

'I've got to go to hospital for some tests. Even if we're not in the same ward. . .'

'They'd never put children and grown-ups in together,' interrupted Poppy.

'No. Still, I might be able to spy the layout of the land.'

'Yes,' agreed Poppy. 'Sorry you've got to go into hospital.'

'Me, too. Boring, boring.'

Poppy remembered that the whole Great Escape Plan was designed to give Will something exciting in his life, and went quiet.

'My darling?' Poppy's mum put her head round the door. Her eyes and cheeks were red, her hair wild but she looked happy.

'I've got to go.' Poppy told Will.

Irena came in and lay on the sofa. 'I was thinking: when I first met your dad. It was in a pub – I went to pubs once in a blue moon – and he was singing. That Karaoke thing. He has a beautiful voice. He was singing for a bet, I learn later. A blue moon for him too. But it was his voice I fell in love with. First of all.'

'Oh, Mum.' Poppy felt embarrassed. She wished her mum had more friends so that she could tell *them* this sort of thing.

'Sometimes, after we were married, I persuade him to sing while I play the piano. You remember this, Poppy?'

'No,' said Poppy firmly.

'Too young, perhaps.' Irena sighed. 'Happy times. Men must always work hard, Poppy. You know this. Particularly big men like Frank. Otherwise things go wrong.'

'Yes,' said Poppy. She knew this would be a good moment to ask her mum about Big Frank going to court and pleading guilty but she couldn't face it.

'I've got to go and do my homework,' she said, and she went upstairs and flung herself on to her bed.

Chapter Thirteen

School had become a strange place for Poppy. In the past she had been hard-working, confident and friendly. Teachers had liked her, she was respected and life had been fun.

Now she couldn't be bothered to please anyone. She didn't looked anyone in the eye, and expressed no regret when she was put in the Black Book for not doing her homework three evenings running.

Eventually, she was sent to Mr Hannigan, the headmaster. He was fairly young and jaunty. Poppy's heart ached because he reminded her of her dad. Then she felt bitter because he was outside in the world and her dad was locked away.

'We're all very sympathetic to your situation,' began Mr Hannigan.

My dad's in prison, why don't you say it? thought Poppy, trying not to cry.

'We want to help you, but I'm afraid we can't do that without your co-operation.'

The only way you can help me is by getting my dad out, thought Poppy, twisting her hands behind her back so hard, they hurt.

'If you don't do your work, you'll fall behind. Do you think that's what your dad wants?'

Unable to control herself any longer, Poppy burst out, 'Nobody cares what he wants. If they did, they wouldn't have put him in prison!'

Mr Hannigan looked down at his tidy desk, moved a few papers so they were even more perfectly in line. He looked up again. 'I am afraid prison is sometimes necessary.'

'Not for my dad!' wailed Poppy. 'He's done nothing wrong!'

'I see.' Now the headmaster was looking acutely uncomfortable. 'I'm sure your mum has talked it through with you.'

Poppy was silent. She couldn't say that her mum had 'talked it through'. 'Yes,' she said – it seemed easier. 'We're going to visit him in prison again on Saturday.'

Mr Hannigan nodded gravely. 'There is one other thing.' He paused. 'You're seeing a bit of Angel Smith. Now I know you have – er – certain things in common – but Angel is older than you and has not had your advantages. His attitude to school will not help his future.'

Poppy almost laughed. She certainly couldn't see Angel listening to Mr Hannigan.

'He is only eleven, of course, but I'm afraid he's already going in the wrong direction.'

Poppy pictured Angel in the prison holding his baby brother. 'I like him!' she said defiantly. 'He understands.'

'Naturally. Yes.' Mr Hannigan leant forward. 'But don't give up all your old friends. And just try and get a bit more work done. Things will improve, I promise you.'

'Yes,' said Poppy, because he seemed to be expecting an answer.

'That's all, then.' He stood up, obviously relieved.

Poppy knew he was trying to be kind but, as she walked away, all she could think of was her visit to prison the next day. Her mum had told her that it was something called a 'family day' when you stayed longer and got to do things in a big hall. When she'd asked what you got to do, her mum had said irritably, 'I don't know. Painting or something. Not riding a bicycle or playing a piano, that's for sure.'

It seemed to Poppy that spending hours with her

parents in a big hall was not likely to be much fun.

It was different going to the prison a second time; just knowing where the visitors' centre and the lockers were made things easier.

There was the usual atmosphere of dismal anxiety. A woman with twin toddlers had just whacked one of them, and he was bawling.

It was nice to see Angel, as usual, carrying round his baby brother. His mum looked glamorous in a white lacy blouse (no wonder she didn't want to carry the dribbling Gabriel) and his little sister had her hair tied up with gold thread. Even Angel had a glinting chain round his neck.

'You look as if you're going to a party,' said Poppy.

'Celebrating, aren't we. He's out Thursday. Last visit.' Angel winked. 'For this round.'

Poppy looked at her mum's pale, wistful face. The only jewellery she was wearing was a medallion of the Virgin Mary. Poppy wondered if Big Frank would go in and out of prison lots of times, and whether she'd get used to it. Somehow she didn't think so.

'How's your Great Escape?' whispered Angel, his mouth half-hidden in Gabriel's curly hair.

Poppy shook her head.

'Going nowhere?' suggested Angel.

Poppy looked at his confident face and knew that he'd never really believed in her plans. 'Don't know,' she muttered, and turned away to look for her mum.

'Where've you been?' Irena pushed her hair back from her hot face. 'It's so crowded and noisy today. It's not that I don't like kids, but this isn't the best place for them.'

'You said it was family day,' said Poppy. 'I suppose their dads want to see them. Why don't you sit down?'

It felt better being protective of her mum. Better than being cross. She took out a book and began to read.

'You'll have to put that in the locker,' said Irena.

'But then I'll have nothing to do.'

'I know. I know.' Her mum patted her hand.

'Give me the key and I'll lock it away, Mum.'

As Poppy went to the lockers, she realised she was dreading seeing her dad. Last time the whole thing had been such a shock – the dogs, the searching, the unlocking and locking – that she'd hardly been able to take it all in. But now she knew about the prison, and Will was in hospital, and the Great Escape was going nowhere, she'd see her dad more clearly.

He was still innocent, though, she reminded herself, even if he had to plead guilty, for whatever reason. Would she dare ask him about that?

➤ ➤ ➤

It took longer to get through the prison than it had last time.

First of all, they were very thoroughly searched – including inside her mouth, which was worse than the dentist rummaging around. Then she had to take off her shoes and she was patted all around her legs which she didn't like at all. Her mum squirmed so much that the female prisoner officer said sharply, 'Mind I don't strip-search you.'

'What's strip-searching? asked Poppy.

'You *are* green,' said the woman with an unpleasant smile. 'Ask your mum.'

But Irena wouldn't answer, murmuring, 'It's humiliating, Poppy. That's all.'

The dogs were less controlled too, frolicking about all over the place. One jumped up at a three-year-old, who began shrieking with terror.

'Not an animal-lover, is he?' joked the handler. This so infuriated the mother of the boy that she let loose a stream of swear words.

Instantly she was surrounded by officers who grabbed her arms on both sides, which made the three-year-old shriek even louder.

'It was the dog's fault,' began Poppy.

But her mum took her hand and led her forward. 'I expect they're nervous because there are so many of us,' she said, adding under her breath, 'Bastards'.

Poppy had never heard her mum swear in her whole life, and was so shocked that she gasped, 'Mum!'

'I am so sorry. I thought I say it only in my head.'

They walked on. Groups of ten were being led across a courtyard with a guard behind and a guard in front. There were high wire fences on either side and walls beyond. The smaller children obviously thought they were in a kind of playground – they kept trying to escape, and were recaptured by bigger brothers or sisters.

'Lucky things,' said Irena, as one little girl shot out from behind her mother and nearly tripped up a prison officer by diving through her legs. 'At least they're having a good time.'

Poppy was remembering what the prison had looked like from the outside when she and Will had prowled round it. Now Will was in hospital and here she was behind at least two sets of walls. She looked and saw first the sky, a square of blue above her head, and then the narrow barred windows in the buildings all round. Not much of the sky to be seen from those buildings. And how stupid to think that a big man like her dad could ever get out through one of them! That man who escaped must have been a lot smaller – or the windows a lot bigger.

'Oh, look!' Two small birds had suddenly flown from the park beyond the walls and were circling above the yard.

'Sparrows,' said Irena without much interest. But to Poppy, they represented freedom. She felt tears forming in her eyes and blinked hastily.

Chapter Fourteen

'Well, here we are again, then.' Big Frank gave Poppy a warmer hug than last time, but he still didn't lift her off the ground or swing her around.

'Hello, Dad!' Poppy found herself blushing because, despite everything, it was so nice to be with him.

'Where is your beautiful hair, Frank?' exclaimed Irena in horror. His curls had been cut off, and what remained was cut close to his head.

'There was a barber in,' said Frank indifferently. 'It gave me something to do.'

Poppy missed the curls, too. Without them, her dad looked more ordinary.

'Poppy's got enough for the two of us,' Frank smiled, as he pulled out one of her long curls and then let it spring back. 'Now, where's all this "activity" we've been told so much about?' He looked round the big hall, gradually filling up with hoards of children. They were more cheerful now, hugging their dads and showing off. 'There was even some talk of football,' added Frank.

Poppy made a face and her mother frowned. 'OK. No football. There's no room for it anyway.'

At that moment, a woman approached Poppy with a pile of pads, pens and pentels. 'There you are, dear.' She was a motherly woman squeezed into a tight purple T-shirt. 'How about Dad, then? Is he into art?'

'I am *not* into art,' grimaced Frank.

'More the macho type, are we,' said the woman, smiling and moving on.

Somehow her cheery warmth left them all feeling better. They found a table and settled round it.

'Go on, Mum,' encouraged Poppy, 'You're the artistic one.' It was true: Irena didn't just play the piano, she could draw beautifully, too – not that she ever had time. Sometimes, Poppy wondered whatever her parents saw in each other, with her dad such an outgoing character and her mum so private and talented. Perhaps coming from different countries meant they didn't really have to understand each other.

'I'll tell you, Popsicle, my darling' – her dad was definitely making more of an effort this visit – 'you and I will write a story and your clever mum can do the pictures. Who knows? Maybe we'll get it published and make our fortunes.'

'Oh, Frank,' protested Irena, but she was smiling.

'We'll take turns, Pops and me. Two lines each. I'll start:

One day a sleek black rat peered out of a hole. "Why does everyone hate me?" he said, and twitched his whiskers crossly.'

Poppy thought hard: '"*Because you're a thief and a bully," squeaked a mouse bravely, before darting away. "And a coward," hissed a snake from the long grass.'*

'Slower, slower,' said Irena, who was drawing as fast as she could. 'Drawing three animals takes much longer than telling their story.'

'Shall I get drinks?' offered Poppy. When she came back after fighting her way through a long queue, her mum had produced a page of brightly coloured animals: a rat in a flashy suit, a mouse in outsize trainers and a snake wearing a baseball cap.

'That's brilliant!'

'*Seeing the snake,*' her dad continued, '*the rat shot down his hole. He sat in the darkness and thought, "I shall go on a charm offensive so that I can be loved like everyone else."'*

Poppy carried on: '"*Perhaps my smart suit puts*

119

people off," *Rat thought. So he dug about till he found a pair of tattered jeans. He had to hold his nose as he put them on because they'd been near some badger poo, but he decided it was worthwhile if it made him more likeable.'*

'I don't think you can say "badger poo" in a book,' objected Irena, her pencil poised above the paper.

'Nonsense,' Frank waved his hand, 'a touch of raw reality is always popular with publishers.'

Poppy knew that her dad hardly ever read a book and probably had never met a publisher but didn't say anything because, unbelievably, they were having a good time. In fact, she couldn't think when they had had such a good time at home. Usually they all did their own thing, which meant she read, Irena made music and, if Big Frank was in, he was on the telephone or the computer or watching TV – in other words, what he called 'working'.

'The first day Rat went out in his new look,' continued Frank, *'he had the misfortune to meet the Wise Owl. "I think you've forgotten to dress properly," hooted Owl, who was correctly attired in a waistcoat and watch chain.'*

Poppy: *'"It's my more relaxed look," growled Rat. "Hmm," said Owl. "You may not realise it but you smell awful, too," and he flew away.'*

Frank: *'Not a big success, thought Rat, but I mustn't*

give up. So he walked on, trying his best to squeeze his mean mouth into a charming smile.'

Poppy: ' "Ugh. Ugh. Ugh." Rat hadn't noticed a Mother Rabbit with six baby bunnies in a patch of daisies. "Please go back to your hole, Rat," said Mother Rabbit, "before my kiddies catch a nasty disease off you." '

Frank: 'So Rat went back to his hole, quite depressed. He realised it wasn't easy to be liked and decided to sleep on it.'

Poppy: 'The next morning he remembered something his mother had taught him: if you want to be liked, be helpful. This seemed easy, so, changing back into his nice clean suit, he left his hole once more to find someone who needed help.'

Frank: 'What should he see straight away but a very small squirrel carrying a very large nut! "May I help you, young Squirrel," said Rat in what he hoped were kindly tones, "to carry your nut wherever you wish to go?" '

Poppy: ' "Aarghh! Eeeech!" cried the squirrel in terror, and, dropping the nut, fled up the nearest tree. "Maybe my dear mother got it wrong," thought Rat, and even more depressed, returned to his hole.'

'This is the best story, I've ever heard', interrupted Irena.

'Poppy looks as if she could go on and on,' said

Frank, looking pleased, 'but I'm storied out. Why don't you write it down, Pops, as much as you can remember, then we can continue another day.'

So Poppy took some paper and a pen and began to write. As she scribbled, her mum and Dad talked. Soon it was time for a snacks-and-sweets lunch.

When Irena went for coffee, Poppy sat closer to Big Frank. She didn't want to spoil the friendly atmosphere but she did need to ask him.

'Dad, you still want to get out, don't you?'

His face, which had been relaxed, became fixed – until he decided to make a joke of it.

'My darling Pops, you can hardly imagine the joys of being in here: no shopping, no cleaning, no working, no boring demands from my wife and daughter – in short, no worries! Why would I want to leave such a paradise?'

'Oh, Dad,' said Poppy reproachfully.

'Oh, Dad!' Frank imitated her. 'That's what I mean: demands. I've only just got settled in, hardly time to recognise my cell-mate by his smelly feet – and he's swapped for one who snores. And now you want to get me out!'

Poppy stared at her dad's big fake-cheerful face. She sighed, and wondered whether he would ever answer her seriously. 'But after you appear in court, you might be out anyway. Mightn't you, Dad? Mightn't you?'

Big Frank's face suddenly changed from humour to blackness. Poppy shrank back. Her dad shouted – or it felt like shouting, although it was probably only a loud whisper, 'You're only a little girl, Poppy. There are some things you can't know and you wouldn't understand if you did. Just take in this: I'm here in prison – and here, unless you provide me with a pair of wings, here I'm going to stay!'

Poppy couldn't say a thing. She knew she was trembling and tears were beginning to fall down her cheeks.

'What is happening?' Irena came back with the coffee and looked from father to daughter.

'Oh, it's my fault.' Frank flung himself back in his chair. 'All this pretending to be Happy Families . . . I couldn't keep it up.' He looked at Poppy, frowned, but said nothing.

Irena set the coffee down carefully and sat facing her husband. 'Just now we *were* happy,' she said. 'Even in here.'

Poppy stopped crying. She had never heard her mum stand up to her dad like this.

There was a silence. Poppy's dad looked at her again, but this time with a sorrowful face. He leant forward and wiped away her tears with his big finger.

'Forgive me, darling. If you can. You're the best daughter in the world, do you know that, and I'm the worst dad. Can you forgive me?'

Instead of answering, Poppy flung herself into his arms and, even though he was thinner, it felt a very comfortable place to be.

'That is better,' said Irena, nodding. 'Now drink your coffee, Frank, and we will all be happy together again.'

So that is what they did and, although at first her fingers shook, Poppy carried on writing down the story. Just as she finished, Angel appeared with his little sister Seraphina, and Poppy read the story to her.

'More! More!' Seraphina clapped her hands and laughed so much that they all began to laugh too, even Frank.

'How many more times can I read it?' gasped Poppy after the third time.

'More! More!' Seraphina cried, until Angel became embarrassed.

'Just say no,' he advised, 'or she'll make you go on for ever. *More* is her top word.'

None of them had noticed how late it was. Suddenly a lot of new prison officers came into the room and the friendly, purple T-shirted woman took away the pentels and paper. 'I'll make sure you get back your story at the other end,' she said, looking at it admiringly.

'I expect to hear more about the rat,' said Frank to Poppy as they hugged.

'Yes,' Poppy agreed. She tried to be cheerful. 'And I can read it to Seraphina.' Then she remembered that Seraphina's dad would be out of prison next time she visited, so she wouldn't be able to read it to her. But she didn't say anything. No point.

Chapter Fifteen

Poppy went to visit Will. Her mum came with her to the hospital.

'I'll take you up to the ward,' Irena said, as they stood together in the busy reception area. 'Then I'll go on to the prison. Can you last out for two hours?'

'Yes, Mum,' said Poppy, although she couldn't think what she and Will would do for so long. 'I can always read a book.'

'Or play a game on your Nintendo,' said Irena encouragingly, which was odd, because she usually preferred her to read a book, however often Poppy told her about games like Brain Trainer II. Irena pushed Poppy ahead of her into the lift which was already bursting with people, including a boy on crutches and an old man in a wheelchair.

It was a relief to be out of the lift and heading down more corridors to the ward. Poppy was glad not to be searched like she had been in prison, mouth open, legs apart, or herded into groups by suspicious screws.

It had made her feel guilty, as if she'd done something wrong.

'There he is!' Irena waved towards a bed at the end of a long, wide room. 'I might be less than two hours.' She gave Poppy a quick kiss and turned back the way they'd come.

Will was playing with his Kindle when Poppy reached him.

'Oh, hi,' He threw it to the end of his bed.

'Hi. You seem OK,' said Poppy.

'Bored, that's all, bored. They've done the tests, but I'm still here.' He scrunched up his pale face into an expression of acute boredom.

Poppy laughed. 'What's wrong with you?'

'Heart. I was born with a bad heart. I'm not even going to talk about it or I'll die of boredom. Instead of dying of a bad heart.' He laughed.

Poppy thought, they'd been in the same school for years and she'd never known it was a bad heart that made him odd. 'Will you be all right?'

'Don't worry. They'll fix it. They always do. Anyway, don't let's talk about it any more. How's your dad? What's the news? I did some more drawings.' He leant over to the locker by his bed and took out several sheets of paper which he thrust towards Poppy.

She sat down and looked at pictures of the prison, of courtyards and walls, of buildings with slit windows, of prison officers and prisoners, of visitors and dogs. 'They're brilliant!' she exclaimed. 'You're *so* clever!' Which was true. Will drew incredibly well. 'The only thing is,' she added, 'everyone looks a bit too cheerful, as if they're in a holiday camp or a shopping mall.'

'Oh.' Will looked so disappointed that Poppy immediately regretted her honesty.

'I've got some drawing for you to do,' she said quickly.

'What?' asked Will, unconvinced.

'When we were in prison, my dad and I started writing a story for kids and we need pictures for it. My mum did some lovely drawings, but they were taken away.'

'What's the story about?'

'It's called "The Rat Who Wanted to be Liked".'

Poppy told Will the story so far. When she'd finished, Will lay back in his pillows and frowned.

'I'm just like that rat.'

'Don't be silly.'

'Yes, I am. Before your dad went into prison and

we made friends, no one wanted to be with me. I quite understand Rat's p.o.v.'

'So you will do the pictures?'

'Sure.' He paused. 'Does Rat make some friends in the end?'

'Oh, yes!' said Poppy eagerly, although she hadn't thought how the story would carry on.

'Let's get started, then.'

Just as in the prison, the time shot by once they entered Rat's world.

'Rat decided people would like him if they felt sorry for him. "I'll put a big bandage on my head," he said to himself. Then he poked his head out of his hole.

Mother Rabbit, running past with her baby bunnies, stopped for a moment. Her bunnies stared. "There's wicked Rat pretending to be hurt," she said, and hurried them by.

Poor Rat retreated into his hole. Since nobody else would, he felt very sorry for himself.

Just then, he heard a loud shriek above his head. He took no notice because he was safe – and it wouldn't be a friend of his because he had no friends. So it wasn't his problem.

Then he thought, that was the whole problem. He had no problems because he wasn't a very nice person. Well, that's what people believed.

Cautiously, he put his nose out of the hole. His whiskers quivered. . .'

'Stop!' said Will, who'd been scribbling away. 'I'm done. Got to have a break. Let's carry on another day.'

Poppy looked up and saw her mum striding towards them.

'Quick!' She gathered up Will's drawings and put them in his bedside locker. 'Keep it a surprise,' she explained. She didn't want to hurt her mum's feelings.

Hardly stopping to say 'Hi' to Will, Irena took Poppy away.

'How's Dad?' asked Poppy. But her mum didn't answer until they were at the bus stop, and then it was with another question.

'You love your dad? Yes?'

'Oh, Mum.' Poppy was sure other kids' mums didn't ask things like that. But then, other kids' dads weren't in prison. Well, not that many. 'Course I do.'

'Yes. Yes.' Irena stopped talking again until they were on the bus. Then she said in a bright tone, 'Would you like to live in Poland?'

'Poland!' Poppy was as shocked as if she'd suggested living on Mars.

'Poland. My home. Where I was born. You are half Polish, you know.' Irena looked offended.

'But Mum—' Poppy began, and stopped. She was going to say, 'What about my friends?' But who were her friends? Will in hospital? Angel?

Instead she said, 'England is my home.' She'd only been to Poland once, when she was too young to remember. Her mum couldn't be serious. She wanted to shout, 'What about Dad?'

'You are right,' Irena muttered gloomily. 'My job here too.'

Poppy looked up, 'This is our stop,' she said.

That evening Angel rang. Poppy wondered how he'd got her number.

'Hey, you.'

'Hi.'

'Guess what?'

'What?'

'My dad's back inside.'

'But he's only just out!' Poppy exclaimed.

'Yeah. One day. Bad scene. Breached his licence first evening.'

'What's that?'

'Places he's not allowed to go. He went. My mum's not happy.'

Poppy couldn't think what to say. Angel always seemed so in charge of things, but now he seemed to want help. 'That's terrible,' she said. 'I'm so sorry.'

'Yeah. Thought I'd tell you.'

'Yes,' said Poppy. There was a silence. 'I'll see you tomorrow.'

'Yeah.' In the background she heard Gabriel wailing, then shrieks from Seraphina.

'Got company,' she said.

'I'm entering them for the X-Factor,' said Angel – and they both laughed.

Chapter Sixteen

'So they're both inside again,' said Poppy to Angel. They were together in their special spot at the far end of the playground. Other children seemed to leave them alone.

'Police car, lights whirring, sirens shrieking.' It was almost as if Angel was boasting. 'My dad's a dangerous fella.'

Poppy thought, this is a really wild world I'm getting to know about. First-hand, not through films or TV. Then she thought, but my dad's not like that. She didn't say it to Angel, though, because it would have seemed rude.

'It's drugs, isn't it,' said Angel, in a casual voice. But Poppy could see he was upset. 'Where I live, everyone starts so young, using, dealing. I had an older bro, you know. Mum was only sixteen when she had him. Took an overdose, didn't he.'

'What do you mean?' asked Poppy.

Angel ran a finger along his throat. 'Things

happen. Bad things.'

'That's terrible,' said Poppy and added, half to herself, 'I wonder what they think my dad did that was so bad.'

'Dunno.' Angel looked embarrassed and shifted uncomfortably in his trainers – big black ones that looked more like school regulation but were probably just as expensive as the silver and blue ones. 'It's always drugs. Or drink. Or both.'

'I mean, what was bad enough to get him caught, even when he's innocent?'

Angel didn't answer this and Poppy didn't say anything either, and soon they drifted apart.

For the next few days, Poppy tried not to think about her dad. Will was still in hospital because it had been decided he needed an operation. 'Only a little one, this time,' he'd told Poppy bravely. This left her two choices: to be alone or to let her old friends come back.

'Want to see my new game?' Jude caught up with her on her way to school.

'That's terrific.' Together they bent together over the Nintendo.

'I don't believe it!' shouted Jude, as she crashed out of the game.

'My turn!' Poppy was so relieved at being back with the girls that she was louder and more giggly than she'd ever been before.

The day seemed to go quickly too, as she walked around the school with Jude's and Amber's arms wound round her. She couldn't get close like that with Will or Angel. They were boys, weren't they.

Every break, the girls gathered in a huddle and no one mentioned prison once.

'Want to watch *Dr Who* at my place?' asked Jude on their way home, and Poppy agreed eagerly.

'Can't imagine anything better.'

'Stay the night, too?' asked Jude and, although they were not usually allowed sleep-overs during the week, this time both their mothers gave permission.

It was a beautiful evening and they went straight out to the garden.

'Let's jump,' suggested Jude, and they raced towards the big trampoline.

'Higher! Higher!' shrieked Poppy. The slanting sun dazzled her eyes, and her legs shot up and down like pistons.

'Let's hold hands!'

Up and down they went, mostly together, sometimes getting out of time, before tumbling down and rolling about on the springy surface until they found their feet again.

Poppy felt she could jump for ever. Her curly hair came out of its band and jumped with her, her breath was mixed in with laughter. It was as if the last few weeks had been a nightmare, not real at all.

'You two mad girls, I've put drinks and biscuits on the table outside!' Jude's mum, Sally, shouted at them.

Reluctantly, Poppy got off the trampoline and followed Jude.

'Hey, lazybones.' Jude kicked the leg of one of her brothers who had just leant over to help himself to one of their biscuits. 'Get your own.'

'Hi, Poppy. Nice to see you around.' Ben smiled at her.

Next morning was the same: happy, ordinary life and no mention of prison.

At school too, Poppy felt she was moving and breathing more freely. She even managed to listen in Miss Bavani's lessons.

'We're going to the seaside this weekend,' said Jude, as they walked home together. 'Want to come?'

'Brilliant!' agreed Poppy without a second thought.

It was only when she got home and Irena said, 'I suggest we set off a bit more early tomorrow, try to get ahead of the crowds,' that she remembered Saturday was prison-visiting day.

'Not me,' she said airily. 'Jude's asked me to the seaside.'

They were standing in the kitchen, but now Irena sat down. She put her head in her hands.

'Can't wait to swim,' said Poppy, turning to go out. 'Have you seen my costume anywhere?'

Upstairs in her bedroom, she fought fiercely not to feel sorry for her mum or picture her dad's disappointment if she didn't turn up. In the end, she found a book to take her mind off it and went to sleep early, without even saying goodnight to her mum.

Some time later, she felt her mum's presence in the darkness closing the curtains and brushing the hair from her hot face. 'Goodnight, my darling.'

''Night, Mum.'

The sea was like the trampoline; it took Poppy's mind

137

off her dark troubles; all she wanted was to enjoy herself.

'Watch out, Pops!' It was odd hearing the nickname shouted out that only her dad used. Rico, Jude's younger brother, came hurtling towards her on his surfboard. She dived swiftly out of the way, laughing delightedly as bubbles blew up into the blue sky.

Jude joined her. 'I can't think why it isn't raining. It always rains when we come to the seaside.'

Up on the beach, Sally was laying out an enormous Italian-style picnic: cold pasta, salami, olives, long sticks of crunchy bread. There was even a tablecloth and real cutlery.

'You'd think my mum was Italian rather than my dad,' said Jude, as they paddled out of the sea and strolled towards the food.

'It's just like Dad's restaurant,' mocked Rico, giving his mum a hug.

'Wipe the sand off your hands,' said Sally, handing them a packet of tissues.

Poppy lay back on the sand, eyes half-shut, stomach filled with delicious food. She'd never felt so contented.

'Sure you've had enough?' asked Sally.

'We're stuffed,' said Ben, which seemed to please his mum. 'Anyone ever told you you should become a pro?'

And everyone laughed, because Sally had been a professional cook when she first met her husband and still worked when she could.

Poppy thought lazily that even in the good times, life at home hadn't been like this.

'I want to stay here for ever and ever,' murmured Jude.

'Me too,' said Poppy in heartfelt tones. 'Your family's so great.'

'You *are* going to stay the night, aren't you?' said Jude.

'I'd love to,' answered Poppy. Then, finding new energy, she jumped to her feet and shouted, 'Race you to the ice-cream man.'

'Wait! I'll get some money from Mum.' Then they were off, speeding across the sand, dodging sunbathers and boys kicking balls.

'I won!' cried Poppy.

'But I've got the money,' replied Jude, and they both took their place in the queue for ice-cream.

Going home in the car, Poppy fell half asleep.

She felt herself fall against the solid shoulder of Ben, who gave her a friendly shove. Sitting between Jude and Ben, she had never felt so safe. And no one had mentioned prison once.

➤➤➤

'You're not coming back tonight, darling?' Irena's voice was sad and tired.

'No,' said Poppy brusquely. She hadn't rung her mum straight away, even though she knew Irena would be anxious.

'Big Frank sent his love.' This sounded odd. Her mum never called him *Big Frank*.

'Thanks.' Poppy couldn't even bring herself to ask how he was, because she didn't want to hear the answer, which was sure to be depressing. 'I'll see you tomorrow.'

'Yes. I'm glad you had a happy day.'

'Yes. Bye.' Poppy put down the phone. Somewhere in the background Jude was suggesting a game of Monopoly and her mum was saying it was too late.

'Just half an hour, then we'll leave it for tomorrow,' pleaded Jude. 'You can play, too.'

Smiling, Poppy went over to join them.

Chapter Seventeen

Walking across the playground arm in arm with Jude, Poppy saw Angel lounging by the wall. He winked at her and she knew he wanted to talk.

'What's that boy looking at us for?' said Jude, tossing her head. Her ponytail swung in a dismissive way.

'He's looking at *me*,' said Poppy.

'Poor you,' said Jude, and switched them both in another direction.

Poppy didn't even look over her shoulder. At lunchtime, she saw Angel again. He brushed past her where she was sitting among her old friends. When he'd gone, she found a tightly folded piece of paper by her plate. She slipped it into her pocket.

Later, in the toilet, she opened the paper. It was a single sentence with 'A' at the bottom.

'YOUR DAD'S IN COURT ON MONDAY.'

Poppy looked at the irregular capital letters and thought, can't he even do joined-up writing? Then she thought, Jude was going on about this court thing ages ago. So was Angel. It didn't happen then, so why should it now? She tore up the paper into little bits and put them down the lavatory. Annoyingly, however often she flushed, one bit or another floated to the surface.

Crossly, she stamped out of the toilet. She could feel her heart beating fast.

Poppy was spending as much time as she could in Jude's house, or sometimes Amber's. Amber was tall and strong and into all kinds of sports. She took Poppy to her judo class after school one day, and Poppy enjoyed kicking and punching so much that she asked her mum if she could join the class too.

They were in the kitchen, Irena watching her daughter hungrily demolish a large plate of Polish sausage with baked beans.

'I'm glad to see you have appetite,' she said in her usual sad voice.

Poppy looked up briefly. She couldn't help noticing how thin and pale her mum had become. 'It's the exercise,' she said. She thought that even Angel's mum, whose husband was in and out of prison all the time, hadn't let herself go like this. She remembered the white lacy blouse.

'So, can I?' She said.

'What, my darling?'

'Sign up for Judo,' said Poppy impatiently. That was another thing about Mum, she didn't listen. Too spaced out and sorry for herself.

'Is it expensive?'

'Oh, Mum. Do you want me to have a life? Or should I just sit around?' Poppy stopped herself adding, 'Like you,' which of course wasn't true because her mum worked very hard.

'Money is a little difficult.' Her mum wore a horrid guilty look. 'Also, some of my parents find they do not need me for their kids.'

Poppy had gone back to eating heartily to avoid the look on her mum's face, so it took a moment for her to understand.

'You mean. . . ?' She really, really didn't want to say it.

'Some people are not kind.' Her mum looked down at the table and Poppy saw tears in her eyes. 'They think a woman whose husband is in prison is not a good teacher for their kids. I not to blame. . .'

'But that's *so* bad!' Poppy flung down her knife and fork. 'So unfair! So wrong!' She felt her face go bright red. 'Even if Dad's in prison, he's innocent and you've done nothing wrong at all.'

'I am married to him,' Her mum said quietly. 'I choose him. I must know, people think. It is not so unfair. It is how is life.'

'No. No!' shouted Poppy, now up on her feet. 'It is unfair! I hate everything! You are *good*.'

Her mum gave a little smile at this. 'Your dad's family come from Ireland. I only understand later what goes on there. With Frank, too, though he a British citizen.' As usual, when Irene was upset, her English was becoming odd. 'Your dad is not bad man, but he knew bad people. They say they fight for freedoms. Want to bomb and kill. He was only a boy. But it is tempting always if things are not so good to go back find these bad people. Not for politics any more, for money.'

'No. No! Don't say all this. I don't want to hear. I'll shout "bananas and custard" if you go on.' Putting her hands over her ears, Poppy began to repeat at the top of her voice, 'Bananas and custard, bananas and custard,' over and over again.

Her mum stopped speaking. She sighed, and

Poppy stopped shouting.

'You are only a child.' said her mum. 'I will not say a word further, darling. My own darling.'

Poppy couldn't eat any more, but she sat down and drank some water.

'You will see Dad this Saturday?' said her mum, as she cleared away.

'It's Amber's party,' said Poppy, adding quickly, 'I'd better do my homework.'

As she lay on her bed, she thought, it's no wonder I prefer to be at Jude's or Amber's.

Later, Irena came up to say goodnight. She kissed Poppy and then hovered by the door. Poppy pulled the bedclothes over her head.

'Of course you must go to Amber's party. But I wonder. . .' She paused. 'Have you forgotten Will? Today is the day for his operation.'

Poppy gritted her teeth and groaned. Will was part of everything that was horrible. Like Angel was. Was there no way she could just be normal and happy? Like Jude? Like all the others?

'He told me he's had lots of operations,' she said in a muffled voice. 'And this one is a small one.'

'I hope. Poor boy. His mum said he is ready for visiting by Sunday.'

'Fine,' grunted Poppy. And then thought what she didn't want to think: on Monday week Frank goes to court.

All the girls were involved in planning Amber's party, which was to be held in an ice rink; then there was the party itself, an all-girls affair. Poppy had never laughed so much as they slid across the ice, bumped into each other and fell flat on their bums.

'So glad it isn't a swimming party,' they told each other. 'Ice skating in summer's just so glamorous' – and they laughed all the more.

On Sunday, Irena went to Mass as usual, and Poppy went with her. Sometimes her mum let her off, but she knew it made her happy when she went. 'Belief is better than no belief,' she liked to say.

Poppy prayed, 'Make everything be all right,' but she didn't mention her dad's name, even to God.

Afterwards they had a pizza before going on to see Will.

The hospital was even busier than before. Will was

in a side room. He had a tube stuck in him somewhere which led up to a bag hanging from a steel rod. It was very, very hot.

'Hi,' said Poppy.

'Hi,' said Will, sounding much as usual, which was a relief.

'I'll leave you two together,' said Irena.

When she was gone, Poppy said, 'Are you all right?' which sounded pretty silly.

But Will smiled. 'Op's over. That's the main thing. It was the waiting, day after day, drove me mad. But, guess what. . .' He stopped, looking a little embarrassed. 'I finished your story.'

'Oh,' said Poppy.

'The Rat Who Wanted to be Liked', said Will, as if she might have forgotten. 'I got bored of reading and there was nothing else to do.'

'That's great,' said Poppy, who was trying not to remember how she and her dad had first started it that day in the prison.

'I can do the drawings now – or when I feel a little stronger.'

'Yes,' agreed Poppy.

'You can read it if you like. It's on that shelf over there.'

Poppy went over and brought back Will's pad. As she opened the pages and started to read aloud, Will lay back and shut his eyes.

'Only Rat's eyes and nose poked outside his hole but he could see where the screeching was coming from: it was a very small kitten caught by one leg in a very large trap. The steel teeth glittered in the sun.

"Stay still and I'll come and help you."

"Miaaooow," said Kitten nervously, because she didn't trust Rat.

Quietly, Rat pulled himself out of the hole and crawled on his belly towards Kitten.'

Poppy looked up from the pad at Will, 'I like the way it's going.'

'Mmm.' Will smiled with his eyes shut.

Poppy began reading again, 'Rat had just reached the terrified kitten, when a black shadow crossed the sun and they heard the sound of heavy flapping wings.

"Oh, oh. Miaow! Miaow!" shrieked Kitten. 'It's the wicked b-b-buzzard come to get me."

"Sshh. Hold still." Rat knew these traps well, because farmers put them out to catch rats.

"Aaooooww!" shrieked Kitten, thinking he was going to eat her.

But Rat was cleverly lifting the piece of the trap that

had snapped on Kitten. "There, you're free!"

With one bound the little kitten dashed away.

Rat was just congratulating himself on his success when he heard a huge noise above his head and all of a sudden felt a shocking pain in his head.

Buzzard, furious at having lost his prey, had swooped down on Rat with his great sharp beak.

"Oh, oh," groaned Rat. But he knew nobody in the world would come to help him. Inch by inch, he dragged himself back to his hole.

Once there he lay panting in the darkness. The pain was very bad.

He must have closed his eyes for a few minutes, because when he opened them, he thought he was dreaming. Sitting round him were Mother Rabbit, Kitten and all the other animals.

"He's awake," squeaked one of the baby bunnies.

Owl blinked his big round eyes, "You are a hero," he hooted solemnly. All the animals sat up and looked serious. "We are going to present you with the Order of Noble Merit First Class for saving the life of Kitten."

"It's a chocolate button," said Kitten. "Very tasty."

"Oh, thank you, thank you," murmered Rat weakly. "All I wanted was to be liked."

At this, all the animals clapped and Squirrel began

singing loudly, "For he's a jolly good fellow".

*So Rat found out what it was to be liked and have friends
and ever after he was the happiest Rat in the world.*

The End.'

'That's lovely,' said Poppy. But Will didn't answer –
he was asleep – and she crept outside to wait for her
mother, thinking that a happy ending was the best
thing in the world.

Chapter Eighteen

On Monday, Amber brought one of her birthday presents into school. It was a mechanical hamster with the sweetest expression who shot around the floor squeaking. Since toys were forbidden, the girls spent a lot of time in the cloakroom and then the toilets, pretending one of them had a nosebleed.

As Poppy came out giggling, she caught sight of Angel. She turned the other way quickly and when she looked back, he was gone.

That evening, Poppy didn't go home. Her mum rang Jude's mum and asked whether Poppy could stay with them, because she wasn't feeling well. Poppy couldn't help being relieved that she'd avoided a gloomy evening.

On Tuesday, Poppy was hanging around in the

playground at break when she saw Angel coming determinedly towards her. She was on her own, so she decided to stand her ground.

'Hi, Angel. Haven't seen you around.'

He stood facing her, as if waiting for something. Then he shook his head so that his thick hair glinted in the sun. He looked serious.

'I've been busy,' began Poppy, but Angel interrupted her.

'Did you get my note?'

'Note?' said Poppy vaguely, as if she didn't know what note.

'I told you, your dad was in court on Monday,' said Angel.

'Oh, yes,' said Poppy, as if she'd just remembered.

'So I expect you know what happened.' Angel's seriousness was turning into annoyance at her continually blanking him.

'Uhm.'

'I expect,' said Angel in bitter tones, 'your mum told you, so I don't need to tell you a thing and I can get right out of your life like you want, and you can go on having a rave with your real friends. Just say, and I'll be off. It's only a couple of weeks to the end of term and then I'll be gone, anyway. Senior school, isn't it.'

Poppy felt herself going hot and then cold. 'I didn't see my mum last night,' she said.

'No calls or texts?' said Angel suspiciously.

'I was at Jude's.'

'Nice one.' Angel gave her a dirty look. 'You want to know what happened in court, or not?'

'How do you know what happened?' Poppy prevaricated.

'Because my dad thinks I'm a mate of yours, and told my mum. So?' Angel stood four square, daring her to deny this.

Poppy looked down. 'Is it bad?'

Angel's whole attitude suddenly changed. 'Prepare yourself, Bro.' He put out a hand as if to touch her, then dropped it. 'What isn't bad?'

Poppy thought that jumping on the trampoline wasn't bad, splashing in the sea wasn't bad. She looked up. 'Go on. What happened?'

'Five years,' said Angel. 'That's what happened. He got five years.'

Poppy stared at him. She had a burning sensation all over her body as if she was going to explode. She managed to whisper, 'You mean, five years in prison? My dad? Big Frank?'

'He'll serve half that, if he keeps his nose clean.

My dad says your dad was in trouble before. Fifteen, twenty years ago. I don't know. When he was a kid. Bank raids in Ireland. That sort of thing.'

Poppy couldn't answer. Her head was feeling funny now, all light and airy. The next thing she knew, she was lying flat out on the ground. Angel's face was above her.

'He's innocent,' she murmured. She saw other legs gathering around her and more faces peering. Angel's face wavered, then came back into focus.

'We'll have to hurry along your Great Escape Plan, won't we,' he whispered, 'before they ship him out. See you around.' Then he went.

'Poppy fainted, Miss!' shouted a voice that might have been Jude's.

Miss Bavani appeared, looking concerned. She helped Poppy up.

'I was coming along for you anyway,' said Miss Bavani. 'The head wants a word. But it looks as if you need the nurse instead.'

Poppy didn't answer. She wished she was still out of it, unconscious on the ground. She felt her whole body shaking.

'Do you think you're well enough to see him?' asked Miss Bavani. 'He said it was urgent.'

'Fine,' muttered Poppy. She dragged her arm free. What did anything matter? *'Five years, five years, five years.'* The words drummed in her head.

━☀━

'Good morning, Poppy.' The headmaster stood up when they came in, which wasn't normal. He came out from behind his desk and pulled out two chairs. 'Please stay, Miss Bavani.'

Miss Bavani looked at her watch.

'Your mother rang this morning, Poppy. She wanted me to tell you something.'

Poppy lifted her head. 'I know,' she said.

'What?'

'I know. Angel just told me. That's why I fainted. My dad got five years in prison.' Poppy couldn't believe how clear and in control she sounded. She thought, I must be in shock. Then she thought, he's innocent and I'm going to get him out. Since neither the headmaster nor Miss Bavani had anything to say, she said out loud, 'My dad's innocent.'

A further silence. After what seemed a long time but was probably only a minute or two, Poppy stood up. 'Can I go now, please?'

Miss Bavani came to life. She put her arm around Poppy. She smelled of flowery scent. 'Why don't you rest a bit, dear.' She got out her mobile. 'I'll call the nurse and tell her to collect you.' She turned to the headmaster. 'I've got to get back to my class.'

'Of course.' He eyed Poppy in a concerned way. 'Your mother didn't feel up to telling you herself. We'll do everything we can to help you.' He paused. 'He'll probably only serve two and a half years.'

'Only?' repeated Poppy, glaring.

'Yes. Well.' The headmaster fiddled about with papers on his desk.

'I'd rather go back to my class,' said Poppy and she noticed the relief in Mr Hannigan's face.

'Fine. Fine. Perhaps that's best.'

The rest of the day passed in a daze.

'Sit down, Poppy, or you might faint again.' Jude and her other friends fussed over her, which was nice but not really the point.

At last came the moment she was dreading: the end of the final lesson and her mum's pale face at the gates. They walked away quickly, hand in hand.

'I am filled with such sorrow for you, Poppy, my so darling daughter. "It's not your fault. I could not tell you myself. I could not see your beautiful young face and bring to it sadness. The headmaster was kind?'

Poppy didn't tell her mum that Angel had been the first to say those words 'Five years', because the Great Escape was all she had to hang on to now and she had to keep it secret.

Her mum was still talking, two hectic red spots in her cheeks. 'We'll go to Poland for our summer holdays. Perhaps for Christmas, too, and you can learn to ski. So long since I ski. Polish children like to ski. Perhaps Jude may come. Skiing is very good on the Polish-German border.'

But Poppy was only half listening. Angel had mentioned the Great Escape. That must mean he had a plan. She totally forgot how she'd been avoiding him over the last week or two. Now he was the only person she wanted to see.

Chapter Nineteen

'Got it all planned, haven't we.'

Poppy had never heard Angel sound so keen. She and Jude were with him in the corner behind the wall. Jude had seen Poppy going over to him and grabbed her arm.

'Why can't I come too?' she'd said, pursing up her mouth crossly.

'You don't know him.' That had seemed a good enough reason, but then Poppy had added, 'You don't *want* to know him.'

'Yes, I do.'

'You could have fooled me.'

'I want to know him because I'm your friend.'

Jude had been a very good friend lately. But Poppy had never talked about her dad in prison, and that had become all-important again. Did she want Jude to be part of that?

It was Jude who had helped her make up her mind. 'I know Angel's dad's in prison,' she'd said, looking embarrassed. 'I know why you want to be with him. Thing is, Poppy, I just want to make up to you for the way I was when I first heard your dad had gone to prison. Please.'

Poppy had looked at Jude and seen she'd really meant what she'd said. She'd always been her best friend. Maybe she'd be it again. Properly. Not just for having good times at the seaside. They used to talk about everything.

'OK. You're on trial.'

The funny thing had been Angel and Jude's faces when they met. Both wore the same expression of trying hard to be polite – although Jude had tried harder. Then Angel went straight into slouch gear.

So Poppy had just launched in. 'Give us the Great Escape Plan, Angel.' Jude's eyes had nearly popped out of her head but Angel was all fired up.

'I've talked to my dad. Mum too. Got it planned, haven't we.'

So that's where they were now, with Angel hopping from one foot to the other and explaining just how it would happen, and Jude's eyes still a bit wild, and Poppy hanging on his every word.

'It's easy, man. Listen up.'

Poppy and Jude drew in closer like in American

movies. Poppy thought how much Will would have enjoyed this.

'Next time my mum visits,' continued Angel, 'with me and Seraphina and Gabriel—'

'Who are *they*?' interrupted Jude.

'Sshh. His sister and brother.'

'. . .my dad gets all angry because he sees a con eyeing up my mum—'

'She's very glamorous, his mum,' explained Poppy to Jude.

'. . .and throws him a punch. Somewhere it won't hurt too much, as it will be one of his mates. The moment the fights start, all the screws. . .'

'Police officers,' explained Poppy.

'. . .will run to stop it. Gabriel will scream, like he does anyway, and there'll be Armageddon.'

'What's Armageddon?' asked Jude.

'End of the world-type scenario,' answered Angel. 'So in the jumble of bodies piling in and shouting, I quietly lead your dad out. How's that?' he crowed.

'Brilliant!' whispered Jude conspiratorially. 'I've never been nearer to prison than the top of a bus, but I get the picture.'

'What about your dad?' asked Poppy. 'Won't he get punished?'

'Knockback, maybe. Time in the seg, more like. He's used to that. Just doesn't care. He says boredom's the worst thing inside. This will liven things up.'

'What's seg?' asked Jude and Poppy together.

'Segregation unit.' Angel was obviously relishing being the one in the know. 'Underground, empty cell. Just a mattress. Nothing to do. No one to see.'

'That sounds *very* boring,' commented Poppy.

Angel shrugged. 'Gives a man a chance to think.'

Poppy didn't think Angel's dad seemed much of a thinker. But he must be very brave and kind to help out Big Frank, who wasn't even a friend.

'What about the other man?' asked Jude. 'The man he hits for eyeing up your mum. Won't he get into trouble?'

'Probably.'

Jude's eyes glowed. 'Wow!' She was reacting like it was a nintendo game, and Poppy couldn't really blame her.

'We must tell Will,' Poppy said.

'Will?' Jude's face fell.

'He thought up the Great Escape Plan in the first place.' said Poppy defensively.

'Hey.' Angel glanced at his oversized chrome-and-many-dials watch. 'Gotta split. See you.'

'Thanks,' said Poppy, before calling after him, 'Want to come to Will's this evening?'

'Na,' Angel called over his shoulder. 'Hospital and me don't mix.'

Jude took Poppy's arm. 'He's quite something.'

'So he's not "that boy" any more?'

Jude swung her ponytail – this time in favour of Angel.

'Will *you* come to see Will?'

'Suppose so.' Jude looked far from keen.

'If there's two of us, our mums might let us go alone.'

'OK. Just don't ask me to like him.'

Will didn't seem much keener on seeing Jude than she'd been on seeing him. Things improved when they explained the new Great Escape Plan.

The colour came into Will's face as he went through the details. 'Doing it from the inside. That's wicked.' Then he became more thoughtful. 'What happens when he gets out? Your dad, I mean. Where does he go?'

Poppy and Jude looked at each other. They'd been so excited by Angel's plan that they hadn't thought what would happen to Big Frank afterwards.

'I don't know,' admitted Poppy.

'He can't go home to your house,' pointed out Will. 'The police will look for him there right away.'

'Uhmm.' Poppy sucked her fingers and frowned. There was a silence.

'What we need is a safe house,' said Will, 'somewhere the police wouldn't connect him to.'

'If we lived in the country,' said Poppy, 'it would be easy. The country's filled with old sheds where anyone could hide for ages. We could bring him food.'

'We don't live in the country,' pointed out Will.

There was another silence.

Jude said tentatively, 'We do have a shed at the bottom of our garden. You know, Poppy, behind the trampoline. No one ever goes into it now, since my mum gave up her idea of a prize garden.'

'That's good.' Will considered. 'In fact, genius! Easy to sneak him food and bring him into the house for a wash when your mum's out.'

'And my dad and my brothers,' pointed out Jude. But Poppy could see that now she'd been called a 'genius', Jude was looking at Will in quite a different way.

'That's sorted, then,' said Poppy. 'We wait outside and when he appears, get him to Jude's house as quick as possible. Agreed?'

'Agreed!' They all high-fived and for once in his life, Will did it right. 'I only wish I could be with you,' he said wistfully, as Poppy and Jude prepared to leave.

'Maybe you will.' Poppy smiled encouragingly. She was glad *she* didn't have a bad heart and operations and endless time in hospital. 'I doubt Angel's dad can set it up straight away. Just get better quick.'

'Right on!' agreed Jude, and hurried out of the room with all the relief that people feel when they've escaped from a hospital.

Poppy glanced back briefly. 'You know, I think Will was so nice straight away about my dad being in prison because he knew just what it's like to be stuck in a place you don't want to be.'

'Unlike me,' said Jude.

'You're making up for it now.'

Arm in arm, they dashed out of the hospital.

Chapter Twenty

Angel gave daily reports on how the Great Escape Plan was progressing. He and Poppy and Jude gathered in their usual place in the corner of the playground.

One day he gave them a thumbs-up. 'My dad's found a mate willing to take a few punches.'

'Who is he?' asked Jude curiously.

'Wee Widgett.'

'Won't a wee little man be knocked over by your dad?' asked Poppy.

Angel laughed. 'He's called "wee" because he's a giant. Prison humour. Six foot five, seventeen-and-a-half stone. Gym every day, muscles like iron. My dad could use him as a punch bag and he wouldn't feel a thing. That's the idea. Now all they've got to do is to get their visitors coming on the same day. And your mum, of course. They won't tell your dad till the last minute, so he doesn't get worked up.'

Easier said than done. A week passed. The only

new development came after an excited call from Will in hospital.

'I've had an idea. There's sure to be an immediate rumpus when the prison realises your dad's escaped.'

'We can't do anything about that,' said Poppy, 'except get him to Jude's shed as quickly as possible.'

'Yes, we can.'

'What?'

'Bring him to visit me first. The hospital's almost next door to the prison. Then, when things have quietened down, move him on to Jude's safe house.'

This was an inspired idea, and when Poppy told Jude and Angel, they thought so too.

So everything was planned, but still they were waiting for the right day.

Then one evening, Irena started to talk about summer holidays in Poland again and Poppy realised there was only a week to the end of term. They'd taken a picnic tea to the local park. When they'd finished eating, it was late and they walked over and sat on the little children's swings.

'I'm sorry you still don't want to see your dad.' said Irena, swinging gently.

'When are you going in next, Mum?' asked Poppy,

swinging a little higher than her mum. This was a crafty question because she needed to know exactly when her mum was going in for the Great Escape Plan to work.

'Thursday.' Her mum sighed and stood up. 'He tells me they're going to move him out of Grisewood Slops.'

Poppy kicked her legs and swung as high as she could. She thought that here was another reason for Angel to get on with the plan. It had to be Thursday.

On Thursday morning, Poppy and Jude and the rest of their class were on a special outing to Chelsea Physic Garden where they learnt about man-eating plants and plants that could cure deadly infections. 'Kill or cure,' commented Jude wittily.

When they got back, Angel was waiting for them in the playground. 'I've been going mental! Where've you been?'

'Avoiding man-eating plants,' said Jude.

Angel didn't even smile. 'I've got it all set up. At least, Dad's got it all set and Mum's up for it. Then I thought you weren't going to be on the receiving end.'

'Sorry. We couldn't get out of the trip. No way.'

'That's so great,' grumbled Angel.

'I said sorry.' Poppy felt hot and bothered.

'Shut up, both of you,' said Jude. 'We've got to keep our energy for later. Luckily my mum and dad are definitely out and Ben and Rico are both practising in the nets at Lords. You know, cricket,' she added, looking at Angel.

'I know cricket,' said Angel furiously. 'You think I'm thick or something?'

'Course not,' said Poppy soothingly. 'Without you and your family, we'd never get my dad out.'

'Sorry,' said Jude. 'I was the one being stupid.'

'OK.' Angel allowed himself to be calmed down. 'I go into the prison with my mum and the kids. You get there the moment school's over. My dad will kick off as late in the visit as he can. But hurry.'

Straight after school, Poppy and Jude were running to the bus stop. Luckily, a bus came immediately but, less luckily, it had one of those drivers who seemed to be on a go-slow, crawling along so that lights turned red that had been green, and then the bus waited at each stop for ages.

'We'll be overtaken by the bus behind,' moaned Jude.

'We should have left school early,' agonised Poppy.

'And be in trouble, like Angel?' said Jude.

Poppy tried to imagine what was going on inside the visiting room. She pictured it filled with anxious women, cross children and sad, angry men. 'I don't expect a fight's that unusual.'

'What if the screws guess something's going on?' worried Jude.

Poppy stared desperately out of the window. 'All I know is, I'll scream if this bus doesn't go any faster.' She pushed back her heavy tangle of hair from her hot face. 'You have got everything ready in the shed, haven't you?'

'You've asked me that ten times already.' Jude was equally sweaty. 'I've put in one sleeping bag, one torch, one bottle of water, one packet of biscuits – chocolate creams because you said Big Frank liked them – one banana, one apple, one Mars Bar, one chunk of cheese and one book of jokes. I wouldn't mind staying there myself.'

'That's terrific,' said Poppy distractedly. The bus had put on a burst of speed and they were nearly at the prison.

'I just hope Will's end is OK,' said Jude.

'It was fine when I talked to him this morning. He's expecting Dad around four.' Poppy jumped up. 'Here we are!'

Now that the big moment had come, both girls took up position opposite the prison gates, but on the other side of the road. They knew exactly what to do: wait until Big Frank appeared and then escort him to hospital, as if he was an ordinary dad with two girls he'd met from school. They'd even brought a peaked cap to hide his face and red hair.

They planned to walk slowly, casually, not at all as if they were with an escaping prisoner. Once at the hospital, they'd behave just like visitors and wait until they couldn't hear police sirens any more. Probably the police would race around noisily looking for Big Frank. There might even be a helicopter circling overhead. Police liked that sort of thing.

Angel would take a back seat because a boy (particularly one with attitude like Angel) would look more suspicious than two schoolgirls.

From the hospital, Jude would take Big Frank on alone, in case they'd been noticed earlier, and, even cleverer, she would have a second cap (both caps the property of her brothers) so that the tall man with her couldn't be identified on CCTV cameras as the same man who'd entered the hospital.

Jude and Big Frank would then catch a bus straight to her house and go out to the shed.

'I guess we've thought of everything,' said Poppy. But at the back of her mind was the one thing they hadn't talked about: how would her mum react?

Jude glanced at her watch. 'Any time now.' Her voice was a bit wobbly. 'Shall we cross the road?'

'Might be good.'

Poppy shivered, partly with excitement, partly with fear as they prepared to cross. Ahead of them loomed the high walls, the barbed wire, the turrets. Would her dad soon walk out free from all this?

'Look out!' Jude's voice was almost a scream.

A large white van was speeding out of the prison gates. It came straight towards them preparing to turn right.

Poppy and Jude jumped back on the pavement. They watched it flash by with its grim, darkened windows.

'That was a sweat box,' whispered Poppy, when they'd both recovered their breath. She could feel her heart pounding.

'What's that?' asked Jude in a whisper.

'It's the horrible van with cages inside that they use to take prisoners from prison to prison.' A nasty feeling was starting in the pit of her stomach.

Jude glanced at her watch again. 'It's getting late.'

'Plenty of time,' said Poppy, although the nasty feeling was spreading all through her now.

They crossed the road carefully, looking both ways twice. Jude glanced at her watch again.

Poppy's mobile rang. It was Will. 'Any sign of him yet?'

'Not yet,' said Poppy, and turned off the phone.

'I'm dying of thirst,' said Jude.

They both shifted from foot to foot.

'My feet are boiling,' said Jude.

'The pavement's like an oven,' agreed Poppy.

They both avoided looking at each other. Some uniformed officers appeared and one of them stared in their direction. He said something to his mate, who also turned his head their way.

'I think we'd better move a bit further off,' whispered Jude.

'But what if Big Frank comes out?' hissed Poppy.

Jude didn't answer, but walked several yards in the direction of the bus stop. Poppy hovered for a moment, then reluctantly followed her. It had now become 'What if Big Frank comes out.'

'If he comes out now,' said Jude in a horribly flat voice, 'those screws will get him.'

'They'll think he's a visitor!' said Poppy fiercely. She didn't really feel fierce. She felt it was all over. No Great Escape. 'The visitors aren't out yet,' she added, as calmly as she could.

'That's true.'

They stood together, both trying to be hopeful.

'Hi, girls. Waiting for a bus?'

Poppy and Jude turned at the loud voice. A police car had drawn up beside them and a policeman leant out of the window.

'Er, yes.'

'Better to wait at the bus stop, don't you think?'

He sounded friendly enough, but both Poppy and Jude sensed the threat.

'Yes,' said Poppy and as he spoke, she saw what she had been dreading: the first visitors were coming out of the prison. It was easy enough to spot Angel's mum and children. Gabriel was in his mum's arms being chased by Seraphina, who was making him giggle with her silly faces. Then Poppy saw Angel walking dejectedly behind them.

Their Great Escape Plan had definitely failed.

Turning back to the policeman, Poppy said defiantly, 'I'm going to meet my mum.'

The policeman put his head right out of the window until he could see the prison entrance. 'So that's it,' he said, with a knowing smirk. 'OK girls, have a nice day.' The police car drove on.

Poppy and Jude walked towards the gates. Angel came towards them. He stood with hands in his pockets, head down.

'They shipped your dad out of the prison, didn't they. Last minute thing. Too late to tell you. Even your mum didn't know till she was in the visitors' centre. That's the way they do things. Your mum went home.' He kicked the ground a couple of times.

A lot of people were pouring past them now, mostly women and young children.

'We saw the sweat box,' said Poppy dismally. 'It nearly ran us over. I sort of guessed Dad was inside it.'

'Did you?' Jude looked up, surprised.

'Bad scene,' said Angel. 'Story is, he's gone to that nick, can't remember what it's called, on an island.'

'An island!' exclaimed Jude. 'That doesn't sound easy to escape from.'

'Ever the optimist,' muttered Poppy – but Jude had to be right.

'Angel! Angel!' called Angel's mum.

'Got to help with the kids.' Angel sloped off dejectedly.

Poppy's phone rang. It was Will.

'He's been sent to an island,' said Poppy drearily. 'We saw the sweat box. Maybe he even saw us.'

'An island! Like Alcatraz or something? Do you think they got wind of our plans?' Will's enthusiasm seemed as high as ever. 'Why don't you drop by and I'll look it up on the internet. Can't be many prisons on islands.'

'OK' said Poppy glumly. Will had a strange way of making her feel better, but she couldn't see how he could make a prison on an island seem like a good thing. 'Jude and I'll be along in a minute.'

'You really mean an *island* island?' asked Will.

PART TWO

A large white van winds its way slowly up a steep road round the edge of a cliff. Below, a steep drop down to the sea. It is evening, the sun just above the horizon. A strong wind creates patterns of glinting breakers on the water. Instead of rolling steadily in to the shore, they break in all directions, as if there are warring currents under the surface.

The men inside the van can only see this dimly through the darkened windows. They sit uncomfortably in small cage-like cubicles. It has been a long journey. The air is stuffy and smelly. Instead of stopping for the toilet, they have been told to use bottles.

The driver is relieved to see the heavy walls, the moat, the stone archway which herald the end of their journey. The sun is dropping fast and soon it will be night. He drives the van in through the arch and stops.

Several prison officers appear.

'You're late.'

'Paperwork before we left. Usual muddle over how many lucky fellas were joining us for the ride.' The driver stretches, putting his arms above his head.

'Should have four. So it says here.' The officer consults a clipboard.

'Three. Sorry to disappoint.' They both laugh.

'Better let out the cattle, then.' The officer goes to the side of the van.

'Quick as you like.' The driver bends from side to side. 'Cup of tea and I'm off again. And they say prisoners have a bad time!'

They both laugh again in a companionable way.

The door is opened and three men stumble outside. They blink, although it is almost dark in the courtyard. The wind has stayed outside.

The tall man looks up at the sky. He sees the evening star shining brightly. He wonders when he'll see that again.

'Come on, then.' Two officers take hold of the man. 'The quicker we are, the quicker we can all knock off. Might even get a nice cup of tea.'

The tall man takes one more look at the sky, at its velvet softness and infinite horizon. Then he follows the officer to a small brown door.

As they wait for the door to be unlocked, he shakes his hands a little so that the handcuffs sit more loosely.

Chapter Twenty-one

Term had already ended before Irena told Poppy she'd arranged for them to visit her dad in his island prison. 'It's called Her Majesty's Prison Castlerock', she read from a piece of paper, with a look of doom.

Meanwhile Will was recuperating at home, and Jude had gone off with her family for a holiday in Spain. Poppy hadn't seen Angel for ages, until the day before their visit to HMP Castlerock he caught up with her in the street. He sat astride what looked like a girl's pink bike.

'Hey! How's things? Haven't seen you since the Great Escape That Wasn't.' He smiled. 'Bit of a flop, that was.'

'Suppose one good thing is your dad didn't have to go into seg.' Poppy spoke stiffly. Nothing about it seemed funny to her.

''He's in seg anyway,' Angel shrugged.

Poppy was shocked. 'Why?'

'A bad-un tried it on, so he got the boiling water treatment over him, didn't he. My dad doesn't let people mess him around.'

Since Poppy had nothing to say to this, Angel added, with another shrug, 'That's prison, isn't it. How's your dad?

'We're going to see him tomorrow.'

'On the island.' Angel looked thoughtful. 'You know, my dad said there was never a chance of getting him out of HMP G. Slops. Far too many locked doors between him and the big world.'

'Then why did he help us?' exclaimed Poppy crossly.

'Bit of fun, he said. Nice to see kids having fun.'

'Fun!' Poppy felt like hitting Angel. But she wasn't so sure he wouldn't hit her back, and he was bigger and stronger than her. 'I thought you were my friend,' she said instead.

Angel's expression changed. 'Yeah.' He frowned. 'Apologies in order. Just in a bad mood. Too much time. Nothing to do. Hope your dad's OK.'

'Thanks. I'll see you around.' Poppy watched as Angel rode off at speed doing wheelies and skids, until a lorry slowed him down.

'We'll take a picnic,' Irena announced, when Poppy got home.

'We'll need a tent, then,' said Poppy. The weather had been wet and windy for several days.

'What do you mean – a tent?' Irena looked suspicious. 'We are not to stay overnight. I have bought day return tickets on the train.'

'Only joking. I was thinking of the rain.' Poppy knew she was behaving badly – she was nervous about going to the new prison. Will had insisted on looking it up on the internet.

'I can't believe it!' he'd squeaked. 'It's like a medieval dungeon. Makes me shiver just to look at it.'

'Calm down. It *is* my dad in there.'

'On a cliff top above raging seas,' continued Will, 'underground dungeons, secret tunnels down to the beach. Honestly, it's more like Alcatraz than Alcatraz.'

'Is that good or bad?'

'Not sure. Here, I'll read you out some more. It's for lifers – that means murderers, mostly – or men on determinate sentences – don't know what that means.'

Soon Will had given up on the facts and gone back to the thrilling bits. 'In the fifties, a prisoner using knotted sheets got over the wall and escaped. He still hasn't been recaptured, which makes him the longest escapee in the world.'

❧

Poppy decided to try out some of Will's exciting bits on her mum. They were sitting on the 9.35 train from Waterloo to the seaside resort of Blackmore Bay, which was the nearest railway station to the prison.

'Do you know, in 2004 a burglar imprisoned in HMP Castlerock escaped in a laundry van. He used the metal edge of his lighter to cut his way into it, then popped off to see his sick mother.'

'Ssshh.' Irena looked anxiously at the other passengers. They were mostly families, some with buckets and spades or rolled up wind-breaks. They obviously weren't heading for the prison, Poppy thought jealously.

'I was only giving you a bit of local history,' she said to her mum.

'Yes, darling.' As well as making a too-big picnic the day before, Irena had washed her long chestnut hair and set it in rollers. She looked very pretty. She was wearing make-up too. 'At least it's not raining.'

Poppy stared out of the window. 'Not yet. Just windy and cool.' Even so, she'd rather be sitting on a beach than going to a prison.

On the other side of the aisle, three small children and their mum were squeezed into two seats. They didn't have any obvious beach equipment. Perhaps they were going to the prison too. They were already squabbling and their mum looked exhausted. Poppy thought it odd that there'd always been this other world of children with dads – or mums, she supposed – in prison and, if her dad hadn't been sent there, she'd never have known about it. It was a secret world, but not one she wanted to be part of. It was the same kind of feeling she'd had standing on the pavement outside Grisewood Slops and seeing people passing by as if the prison didn't exist.

'If you don't sit still,' said the exhausted mum in a shrill voice, 'I'll tell your dad and he'll have something to say!'

A dad, then, thought Poppy, but that doesn't prove anything either way. She pressed her face to the window.

'What are you thinking, darling?' Her mum put her arm round her shoulders.

'Rain,' lied Poppy. 'Will it? Won't it?'

'Won't,' said Irena. 'Would you like a pastry now?'

'Thanks.' As Poppy munched, the train stopped and more holidaymakers got in. The teenage girls were particularly loud, their lipsticked mouths contorting in laughter. Poppy stared at one with silver-blue eye shadow and a blond quiff and wondered if she'd be like that in a few years. At least they were having fun. Then she wondered if Jude was having fun in Spain.

The train became more and more full as they neared Blackmore Bay. People were standing all along the aisles. Outside the windows, a glint of sun streaked the green countryside.

'There,' said Irena, 'I knew we were going to be lucky with the weather.'

'We're being welcomed to the Jurassic Coast.' said Poppy. She was reading a sign on the station platform. They had arrived.

'And now,' Irena gathered together the bags, 'we must look for a taxi. The bus is infrequent, I'm told, and eight miles is too far to walk.'

'Don't we need a boat?' asked Poppy.

'There's a long causeway to the island.'

The happy crowds passed them, all heading to the beach. Poppy sniffed the sea air, but there were too many cars in front of the station to get even a whiff of salt or seaweed.

They waited over half an hour while another train came in, and eventually a taxi appeared.

'Castlerock, if you please.' Irena bent forward to the driver but he didn't understand her accent.

'The prison,' shouted Poppy defiantly.

The driver turned round to look at them. He was old and hairy, 'Which one?' he asked.

'Castlerock,' repeated Irena, and Poppy saw she'd gone red in the face. They had been able to catch a bus to Grisewood Slops without anyone knowing where they were going.

'That'll be twenty pounds,' said the driver. As if they were thieves and couldn't pay, thought Poppy.

They began to circle the back of the town, passing green spaces and low houses until suddenly, on their right, Poppy saw a harbour crammed with smart white boats.

'Look at that!' She nudged her mum.

Irena, who had been staring downwards, hardly lifted her head. 'Mmm.'

'It's all boats and sailing here,' said the driver.

'Pretty. Pity they can't see it where we're headed.' The driver's eyes twinkled at Poppy in the rear view mirror. 'Would be a grandstand view if it wasn't for those mean old walls.'

Irena didn't answer, and Poppy turned to face the window so the driver couldn't catch her eye again.

Once they'd passed the harbour, the road began to climb. Not much sign of an island, thought Poppy. But a few minutes later, they were back to sea level and there in front of them was the sea stretched out ahead, green and shiny under the clearing sky.

'Famous beach to your right,' said the driver, pointing to a seemingly endless expanse of shingle, 'and Castle Island straight ahead.'

Her mother had been right. A long causeway stretched out into the water, bordered by low walls. At the other end of it, a brooding mass of rock rose steeply. On its lower slopes there were houses but, as Poppy peered out, crouching to look upwards, she could see great cliffs and barren rock.

'Up to the top we go!' said the driver cheerfully.

At the far end of the causeway, on the island itself, the road began twisting sharply upwards. Soon they had left behind the few houses and instead there was grey tufty grass with a steep incline on one side, and on the other, a breathtaking drop to the dazzling sea below

Poppy's hands were sweating and her heart was beating too fast. She could no longer see the top of the island. Then, without warning, they were in a deep cutting in the cliff side. It was lined with heavy slabs of stone covered with yellow netting. It was as if they were entering a giant's lair, or maybe a castle belonging to a wicked king.

'Mum!' Poppy nudged her mother.

The walls had become higher and higher and now they were closing over their heads into a dark and narrow tunnel. Poppy gripped her mum's hand.

'Nearly there,' said the driver.

There was light at the end of the tunnel. Then they were out and facing smooth high walls which stretched away in either direction. Round them circled a deep, dry moat.

'Her Majesty's Prison Castlerock,' announced the driver, as if they hadn't guessed.

Irena scrabbled in her bag for money. Poppy leapt out of the car and took deep breaths. High above her head a single seagull wheeled and cawed. The clouds were moving fast across the sky and the air smelled fresh and pure.

Poppy's mum joined her. She blinked nervously.

'Planning on leaving later, are you?' The driver leant out of his window.

Irena seemed too dazed to answer so Poppy told him firmly, 'We'll be all right, thank you.'

She watched as he drove away, then looked around. There were the walls, outer and inner – she could see the rolls of barbed wire on that one – and more buildings, all built of stone and very grim. She wanted to get a view of the sea, but they seemed to be in a dip.

'Why's no one else here?' she asked.

Her mum stared around vaguely. 'I didn't want to be late. There's the visitors' car park.' She turned one way, and then another. 'And there's the visitors' centre. We can eat our picnic inside.'

'Must we? Can't we stay outside?'

'If you prefer, darling.'

So they sat on a kerb by the car park and tried to eat the huge picnic Irena had prepared. Neither of them felt hungry. Although the air was warmer, an annoying wind kept trying to blow away the wrappings. Poppy threw away a crust and three seagulls dive-bombed from nowhere and fought for it, cawing angrily.

'Don't,' said her mum. 'Look at those beaks.'

'Oh, Mum,' protested Poppy, but she didn't throw any more food away. She thought of having a wander to see if she could see the sea, but there were signs everywhere: *No unauthorised person beyond this point*.

A few cars began to arrive, some people on foot who must have come off the bus and a couple of taxis.

'We pack up now,' said Irena.

Slowly, following the other families, they walked over to the prison.

Chapter Twenty-Two

'So here we are, all together again.' Big Frank's voice was cheery, given the surroundings. Poppy was still a bit dazed after their progress from the visitors' centre (nice and friendly) through the double walls of the prison and across a great green space the size of a football pitch, to the dreary room where they now sat. Not to mention all the security stuff: the searching, the removing of their shoes, the looking inside their mouths, the pat-downs, the suspicious questions. All this, just to see her dad.

Poppy looked at him properly. It was weeks since she'd seen him in Grisewood Slops. Now his face was almost back to its usual brick colour, his hair was growing into curls again, and altogether he seemed more like his old self.

'You look well,' said Irena timidly.

'I'm out in the open air.' Frank took Irena's small hand in his big palm. 'They took one look at this big Irishman and decided to put him to work in the fields.'

'But Dad, you're not Irish,' said Poppy. 'You always say, you were born in England and that makes you English.'

'Frank Maloney, and not Irish?'

'You don't even have an Irish accent.' Poppy didn't want him to be Irish because it somehow linked him to bad things in the past. It was quite enough having a Polish mother.

'Only joking, Pops.' Now Big Frank held her hand. 'You'll never guess what I'm doing outside.'

'Growing vegetables,' suggested Irena.

'Not far off.'

'In a prison?' Poppy exclaimed.

'Grow your own and eat them. Cheap labour, my darling. I started with that but I've moved on now.'

'Go on, tell us, Frank.'

Poppy could see that her mum was as surprised by the change in Big Frank as she was.

'Ducks and chickens. A mate of mine got sick and gave me his job. Never knew what fun it was, taking care of stupid little animals. I have learnt something, too: waddling is a very inefficient way of getting somewhere quickly.'

'That *is* good,' said Irena seriously. 'Maybe we get a cat for when you home.'

Poppy assumed her mum was joking, and laughed – her dad had always said he was allergic to cats – but her dad looked suddenly sad.

'Get us a drink, would you, Pops.'

So Poppy went over to the canteen bar and while she was away, she could see her dad and mum having the sort of intense chat grown-ups have when the children are out of the way.

It made her cross. Perhaps she wouldn't try and get him out of this prison. After all, he seemed perfectly fine until her mum mentioned home. Looking after ducks and chickens, indeed. It sounded more like a holiday!

Poppy plonked down the two cups of coffee and went back for her apple juice. She drank it standing up, looking round the room. Prison wasn't new to her any more, but it still felt horrible. There was the same mix of mums and children, girlfriends and mates, grannies and grandpas. Not many grandpas, actually. And no friendly Angel.

'Come on, Poppy. Sit down with us.' Big Frank patted her chair.

'I've been sitting all day.'

'Yeah. Long way to come for a couple of hours. Glad you did, though.'

Poppy forced herself to sit down, and her dad put his arm around her shoulders. 'Did you ever finish that story we wrote? What was it? 'The Rat Who Wanted to be Loved.'

'Liked,' said Poppy.

'What?'

'Liked, not loved.' He couldn't even remember the name of their book.

'Oh. OK. So did you finish it?'

'Will did.'

'That's her friend Will who had the heart operation,' explained Irena.

'He's fine,' said Poppy, as if her mum had said he wasn't. 'He's done great drawings, too,' she added. She felt cross and impatient. Soon they'd have to say goodbye to her dad and she wanted it to be over now, and be back in the fresh air.

'They ought to have visits outside in the garden,' she said.

'I'll be sure to suggest it to the Governor,' said Frank, trying to humour her, 'or you ask him on the way out, if you happen to bump into him.'

'I'm not an idiot!' exclaimed Poppy.

'Of course you're not.' said Big Frank charmingly. 'You're my beautiful clever darling daughter.'

Poppy looked down. She wanted to believe him and love him. But why had he got himself locked up? It wasn't fair. Not on any one. Not on him, because he was innocent, and not on her mum and herself, either. Maybe she *would* help him escape. Then she thought of the cliffs and the tunnel and the double walls and her heart sank. If Angel's dad was right and they could never have got him out of Grisewood Slops, what hope was there here? She hadn't even asked her dad about the underground dungeons or whether there might be secret tunnels leading off them. Now she couldn't ask, because they were leaving.

It seemed a long walk back across the grassy space at the centre of the prison. Poppy looked up at the sky. It was bright blue.

'The wind's blown away the clouds,' said her mum. 'It's blown itself away too,' she added. She was right. The gusty wind had died away and the only sound was of seagulls noisily cawing and children shouting as if they were on a football pitch.

'I suppose it's better than Grisewood Slops.' Her mum sighed. 'Too far away from London, though.'

'Yes,' agreed Poppy, still staring at the sky.

After that, they were both quiet as they were let out through the walls of the prison and into the car park. After all the effort and fear involved with getting in, Poppy felt a sense of anti-climax. It was all over so quickly. Now here they were with half the day to fill. The sun was hot. Some families had produced food and drink from their cars and were picnicking. Two girls had taken off their T-shirts, revealing bikini tops. It seemed strange to do that so close to a prison.

'I'll tell you what,' said Irena suddenly, 'why don't we have a swim?'

'We haven't got swimsuits.' Poppy stared at her mum. She'd assumed she was thinking sadly about Big Frank, not about swimming.

'I've been meaning to buy you a new one all summer.'

'What about our train?' Surely mums were supposed to be sensible. 'And we've got the long walk down.'

But a car stopped by them just as they set off down the road.

'Want a lift?' A woman leant out of the window. She was quite old, smartly dressed with pearl earrings and a jaunty scarf.

'That is kind.'

'It's hot weather for walking.' She had a sensible, kindly voice. Poppy couldn't imagine her having a son in prison. She got in the back of the car while her mum took the front passenger seat.

'It was cool when we started,' said her mum.

'Come from far, have you?'

'London,' said Irena.

'Me too.' The woman glanced sideways. 'I'm Lennie. I saw you inside.'

'Irena and Poppy,' Irena said.

Lenny smiled. 'That's pretty.'

'She had red hair even when she was born. Like her dad.'

Poppy sat quietly in the back seat. So many things seemed weird today but this chat was the weirdest, just as if they'd all met in a supermarket, not a prison.

'You came by train, then?'

'Yes.' Irena smiled. 'We're not going straight back. We're going for a swim.'

'Good for you!' exclaimed Lennie. 'In all the years I've been coming here, I've never heard of anyone going for a swim.'

Irena actually laughed! Poppy couldn't believe it.

'Something nice for Poppy. Visiting your dad in prison isn't easy.' Poppy didn't want to hear this said to a stranger. She tried to open a window but couldn't find the right button.

'My kids only visit their dad about once a year. It's hard, like you say. Especially when it's a long stretch.'

'Your husband?' asked Irena tentatively.

'A lifer,' said Lennie.

At last Poppy managed to press the right button and shoot the window right down. Warm salty air came rushing in. The road was following the winding curves of the cliff edge and far below, the brilliant blue sea spread up to a paler blue sky. She took deep gulps and felt as if she'd been holding her breath the entire day.

All too soon they were entering the outskirts of Blackmore Bay.

'There's a Marks & Spencer near the front,' Lennie was saying.

'Perfect,' said Irena, adding, as she had at the beginning, 'It is so kind of you.'

'It's cheered me up. I'll give you my number in case you ever need to talk.'

They got out of the car right in the centre of town.

'Quick'. Irena took Poppy's hand and pulled her into the shop.

When they came out, Poppy had a new turquoise bathing suit with grey spots. Nothing for her mum, however.

'I shall write to your dad and tell him all about it.,' And she smiled at Poppy.

'So I'm swimming for my dad,' said Poppy.

The tide was far, far out, exposing a great expanse of sand, some of it still wet, most of it covered with people.

'You'd better change here,' suggested Irena, giving Poppy her suit and holding the towel up. Then they went on the long walk to the water. Around them, children dug holes which immediately filled with water. A group of older children were building a castle with high walls and a moat. Poppy stopped and stared at it.

'You know what that looks like,' she said.

Her mum stared too. 'Prison follow us even to the beach.'

They walked on, water squeezing up from the sand and oozing between their toes. 'It tickles,' said Poppy. 'Like worms.' She looked up, and the glinting water seemed as far away as ever. 'Suppose one day we'll get to the sea.'

'It is funny, I think,' said Irena. 'Here we are trying to be wild and free, and the sea just goes further and further away.'

When they did reach the line of water, it was only a few inches deep.

'Even a starfish couldn't swim in this,' said Poppy. Laughing, she lay down, spread her arms and legs and splashed vigorously.

'I wish I had a camera.' After a few minutes, bundling all their possessions on one arm, Irene looked at her watch. 'Time to give up, darling. Time for train.'

Chapter Twenty-Three

Will opened the door to Poppy.

'You're better!' she exclaimed.

'Nearly better,' said his mum. 'he's got something exciting to tell you.'

Will led Poppy upstairs to his room, walking slowly. They both sat on his bed.

'So tell me.'

'About the prison, you mean?'

'Yes. Yes.' Will sounded impatient.

'But what about your exciting news?'

'I'll tell you afterwards.'

So Poppy began to describe the weird place where her dad was passing his days. The ducks and the chicken and her funny swim. But quite soon, she noticed Will's eyes darting off to a pile of books and papers on a shelf.

'Come on, Will,' she said eventually. 'We can do prison any time. What's the excitement?'

'I was trying to be cool,' said Will. He got up

quickly and came back with a single sheet of paper. 'It's a letter,' he said, unable to repress a smile. 'And it's for you as well as me.' Poppy was about to snatch the letter when Will added, 'Shall I read it aloud?'

'OK.' Poppy wondered if you always had to give ill people what they wanted. In which case, she wouldn't mind being ill herself now and again.

'Dear Will,
Your mother, who is my doctor, has showed me your story "The Rat Who Wanted to be Liked"...'

'It's not your story!' interrupted Poppy.
'Wait.' Will carried on reading.

'I know you wrote it with a friend but I don't know her name...'

'And my dad wrote it too,' said Poppy, frowning.
'Do you want to hear the letter?'
'Sorry. Sorry.' Poppy clasped her hands behind her head and sat back in listening mode.

'I am a publisher specialising in children's books and I like your story very much indeed. I do have a few *thoughts about editing but, subject, to that, I'd like to have first option on publication rights.*

Yours sincerely,

Ivy Underhill'

Will stopped reading and looked at Poppy. He was grinning hugely. 'She wants to publish it.'

'Is that what all the gobbledygook about options and rights means?' said Poppy. She was still frowning, because she was remembering back to when she and her dad had invented the rat story in Grisewood Slops, and she couldn't help thinking how far away Big Frank was now.

'I forgot the P.S.' said Will, looking down at the letter again. '*I like the drawings too, although they may need some work.'*

'Great.' Poppy wanted to be excited, but still felt held back by thoughts of her dad.

'I'm sure your dad would be really pleased,' said Will defensively. 'He doesn't want everything to be bad.'

Poppy considered ducks and chickens for a moment, then said in the same bitter voice, 'He's still innocent, you know. And he's still in prison. But I don't hear you talking about escape plans any more.'

'That's not fair!' Will went bright red in the face. 'I wanted to talk about your visit. It's you who made me tell you the news first.'

'Only because you weren't listening to a word I was saying.'

'If that's how you feel, I'll tear up this letter. What do I care!' With shaking hands, Will began ripping up the letter, flinging bits on the floor.

Poppy watched, horrified. How had it come to this?

They heard Will's mum coming up the stairs. She stood looking in at Will, who was now crying tears of frustration while Poppy sat stunned. Will's mum stared in disbelief.

'Poppy? What's happened'

Poppy felt like crying too. 'I didn't want my dad to be forgotten,' she said.

'I see.' Will's mum went over to him and patted his shoulders.

'It's the letter,' he sobbed.

Poppy thought how brave Will had been all through his operation and afterwards.

'I'm sorry. It's all my fault.' She knelt on the floor and began collecting scraps of paper. Her hands were shaking. She put the scraps on the bed. Soon there was quite a pile. 'We could Sellotape them,' she said.

'I don't know why I was so horrid.'

'Never mind.' Now Will's mum was patting her shoulder.

'I tore them up,' said Will. 'It was my fault too.'

'No worry about that.' Will's mum even seemed to be smiling a little at the children's tragic faces. 'Ivy Underhill's sure to have a copy.'

Poppy went closer to Will. 'I *am* excited about the Rat getting published. I think it's wicked, brilliant, amazing! I just got in a tangle, that's all. Sorry.'

'I'm sorry, too,' said Will, sniffing and grinning.

So Poppy and Will, with the help of drinks and biscuits from Will's mum, began to read out loud to each other, 'The Rat Who Wanted to be Liked.' Soon they were laughing at the good bits and suggesting changes to the not so good.

Unsurprisingly, neither of them thought about prison for one moment.

'I can't believe it,' said Will, as Poppy was leaving, 'We'll be real published authors!'

'It's amazing!'

Poppy ran the two streets home and told her mum the news.

'Oh, darling! Darling!' cried Irena, and burst into tears.

'Mum, it's good news,' Poppy put her arms round her.

'I know. That's why I cry. It is the first good news for so long.' Irena blew her nose. 'Now you will write this to your father and he will be so pleased.'

Poppy pictured Big Frank shaking a pail among quacking ducks and pecking chickens. 'OK.' She thought a bit, then sat down at the kitchen table. Her mum had moved to the stove and had her back to her. 'Mum?'

'Yes, my darling?'

'What is Dad supposed to have done?' She saw her mum's back stiffen. She remembered those first days when her mum wouldn't tell her anything about her dad. Or told her lies. Were they back to that? Would she turn round and shriek?

Poppy sat rigidly in her chair.

Irena turned round. Her face was contorted in an effort to look calm and normal. 'You need never know that. Never. Your dad is good man.' She turned back to the stove and began stirring briskly.

Poppy took a deep breath and realised she didn't really want to know the answer. The main thing was to remember that Big Frank was innocent.

Her mum poured two bowls of soup. She brought

them to the table and sat down. 'Our flights are booked to Poland,' she said. 'They're only a little more expensive than the coach.'

Irena had told Poppy several times about this holiday to Poland but, until now, she hadn't quite believed it. 'Jude's back in three days,' she protested. 'And now there's Will and the Rat book.'

'You will love where we go,' said Irena, spooning her soup with a nostalgic look on her face. 'We stay with my grandparents. They are very old and very kind, in a little village in the country. My brother too will come and my parents not so far away. They will love you so much.'

'I don't speak Polish.' Poppy burnt her mouth on a big gulp of soup.

Irena frowned. 'That is because you were a naughty little girl and wouldn't learn. And your dad did not help. Perhaps now you will learn. I am told there are other children in the village also on holiday.'

'And what about Dad?' said Poppy.

'We will write to him,' said Irena simply. 'And perhaps you will keep a diary. My brother and I will show you the country. My country. Partly your country too.'

After that, Poppy didn't argue. They were leaving in five days, so she still had time to work with Will on the book. She only saw Jude once. They were in Jude's bedroom and she insisted on showing Poppy the line where the sunburn met the white skin under her swimsuit.

'Have you ever seen such a difference!' she exclaimed proudly.

Poppy honestly couldn't see what was so terrific. 'I only go scarlet or freckle in the sun,' she said.

'Poor you,' said Jude with exaggerated sympathy. 'It's such a burden being a redhead.' She considered Poppy. 'Although, really, you're more orange.'

Poppy began to think she wouldn't miss Jude that much.

'I forgot to tell you.' Jude flopped down on the bed. "We're going to Cornwall for a week at the end of the holidays and Mum said you could come.'

Suddenly Poppy felt keener on Jude. 'I'd love that! It'll be something to look forward to while I'm wasting my time in Poland.'

As the time grew closer, Irena grew more and more excited, loading their bags with books and maps.

'I want you to see everything! You never know when we go back again.'

From Poppy's point of view, this was good news.

At last they were off, hurrying down the pavement to the Underground, each pulling a suitcase and carrying a bag on their back. Poppy looked up to the sky and saw puffy white clouds sailing across a blue backcloth. Soon we'll be flying through that, she told herself with shivery excitement.

'Hiya.'

Poppy was about to follow her mum down the steps to the Underground. She turned round.

'Angel!'

'Off somewhere, are you?'

'Poland. My mum's family.'

Angel was astride yet another new bike, this one a flashy purple. The hood of his sweat-shirt was pulled up.

'Coming back, are you?'

'In four weeks.'

'See you around, then.' Angel turned to go.

'Sorry. I'm sorry,' Poppy called after him, then

bumped her case down the steps.

'Whatever kept you?' Her mum was waiting at the bottom.

Poppy didn't answer. Clearly, Angel wasn't going anywhere for his holidays.

Chapter Twenty-Four

Holidays either seem to stretch out endlessly or flash by. The weeks in Poland were so unlike anything Poppy had known before that they seemed like a different time zone altogether.

Every day she woke up to new experiences. Sometimes she and her mum were staying with her grandparents deep in countryside which was so old-fashioned, with its neat little fields and dark forests, that it felt like a fairy tale. Other days, they were in a tiny flat in a tall modern block on the outskirts of Warsaw. The fact she spoke no Polish and most of her relatives spoke no English made the whole experience even stranger.

In all the time they were away, her mum only mentioned her dad when someone asked. She answered in Polish, but Poppy guessed from their happy nods and smiles that her mum wasn't telling them where he really was. As far as she could make out, Irena hadn't even told her close family about prison. She didn't blame her mum. There was no point in them knowing. But it made everything even more unreal.

Her mum was happy, though, which made Poppy happy.

'You like my country?' she asked Poppy when they were visiting a beautiful old city called Krakow. They were eating ice cream in a huge square, waiting to meet some more cousins.

'Oh, yes,' said Poppy. 'It makes me closer to you.'

'That is true. When you are older, I will tell you more history, much very sad.'

'Is that why you live in England?' asked Poppy who'd never wondered about this before.

'Sadness is everywhere,' said her mum, and Poppy knew she was thinking about her dad. Then her mum added firmly, 'Now we are having fun.'

If Polish 'fun' became too much, Poppy picked up her Nintendo or one of the books she'd brought, or wrote in her diary. The diary had become a habit, a friend.

'Well, it was nice to see where my mum comes from,' she wrote on their last day in Poland, 'even if I'm glad to be going home.'

There was only one day left in London before Poppy went to Cornwall. Her mum, trying to cope with the washing, sent her out to buy some milk.

Poppy walked slowly along the pavement. It didn't seem solid under her feet. I don't think my body's quite arrived in London yet, she thought to herself. It can't find my old self who used to walk along these pavements.

'Hi, Poppy,' said Zita in the corner shop. 'Had a good holiday, did you?'

'Fine,' said Poppy, thinking that even Zita look different, her eyes bigger and darker, set off by the scarf drawn tightly round her face. Would everyone seem different now?

While she and her mum were re-packing her bag for the next morning, Poppy asked, her voice a bit quavery, 'Will you be going to see Dad next week?'

Irena jumped, dropped a T-shirt she'd been folding, and said, 'I don't know.'

'How could you not know?'

'I mean to say, it depend on your dad. He hasn't sent a visitor's order. He hasn't...' She faltered to a stop.

'What's a visitor's order?' Poppy's heart was sinking. Was everything to be muddled and horrid again?

'I must have a visitor's order before I can go into the prison. I expect Frank forget.'

'Forgot,' said Poppy. Since Poland, her mum's English had definitely got worse.

She thought of the sea. Cornwall had a very rocky coastline, Jude had told her. They'd leap off rocks into deep water. Not like Blackmore Bay where she'd had to walk for miles over the sand and then the water didn't even reach up to her knees.

'Yes,' said her mum, 'He hasn't written yet, so I expect he'll send the visitor's order then.' She turned back to the packing.

Poppy could have asked, 'Why hasn't Dad written?' But she didn't. 'I'm going to ring Jude,' she said.

'Do it on the landline. It's more cheap.'

'Cheaper.'

'Cheaper,' repeated Irena, sighing.

Poppy and Jude had a thrilling chat about what they were going to do in Cornwall. Then she phoned Will and had a thrilling chat about meeting the publisher Ivy Underhill when she got back to London.

'My heart's responded well,' he told her. 'So I'll be back at school. Can't decide if I'm pleased or sorry.'

'Well, I'm pleased,' said Poppy.

'Thanks. Guess who I saw the other day?'

'Angel,' said Poppy.

'How did you know?'

'Your voice. Everybody uses a special voice when they talk about Angel.'

'Not surprising, considering.'

'Considering what?'

'He had a policeman on either side of him.'

'What!' shrieked Poppy.

'I *think* he'd been arrested.'

'But he's only eleven!,' said Poppy.

'I think he'd stolen something.' Will went on, 'At least, a man by a street stall was standing on the pavement telling the police something or other. It was on Portobello Road.'

'Were you just sitting there staring?' Poppy asked crossly, as if whatever had happened was his fault.

'I was in the car waiting for my mum,' said Will, defensively. 'I didn't want to watch.'

'They can't put a child in prison, anyway.' Poppy sucked her fingers, then her hair, 'I'm going away tomorrow,' she added.

'I know. I wasn't going to tell you. I thought you'd be worried.'

'I am,' said Poppy. But at that moment she began to think of the car journey from London to the far West of England. They were going to stop at an adventure playground on the way. 'I'm only gone for a week,' she said. She pictured Angel on his bike when she'd last seen him, just before she left for Poland. So he *was* spending the holidays in London. Every day of them.

The week in Cornwall was as different as could be from her holiday in Poland. Every minute Jude was there beside her; they shared a bedroom, shared clothes, shared games on their Nintendos, shared books, shared food, jumped into the water at the same time, scrambled out together, lay wrapped in towels on the same rocks, sheltered from the rain together. Watched the same TV programmes in the evening.

Poppy supposed this was what it was like to have a sister, and Jude, who only had brothers, thought so too. The only time Poppy spent on her own was when she wrote up her diary.

'Let me have a look,' Jude asked once.

'It's a *secret* diary.' Poppy replied, although really, there was nothing secret in it. She never mentioned Big Frank, Angel, nor even Will. They could wait until she was back in London.

The week in Cornwall passed quickly. Early on Friday evening Poppy was dropped back at her house.

'See you at school!' Jude shouted, and waved out of the car window as Irena opened the front door.

'My darling! You look so very very well.' Poppy's mum alternated between hugging her so tight she could hardly breathe, and pushing her away so she could get a better look.

'I've only been away a week,' protested Poppy. But it was nice to be home. Her mum had made *blinis*, Polish pancakes filled with sour cream and blueberries and honey.

With her mouth full, Poppy asked, 'Any news?' Then she regretted the question She was not sure she was ready for the answer.

Irena looked down at her plate and didn't answer immediately. Then she said quietly, 'I had a letter from your dad. Two days ago.'

Poppy's heart did a little flip like a pancake in a pan. An image of her dad as he used to be, strong and loud, filled with warmth and good humour, brought quick tears to her eyes. She blinked them back firmly. 'How is he?' She too looked intently at her plate, as if it was more than the remains of a delicious pudding.

'He is good.' Irena spoke slowly, choosing her words carefully. 'His ducks and chickens are good too.'

Poppy felt a hysterical need to laugh, which she managed to suppress.

'He is helping other,' she hesitated, 'other prisoners. It is a special programme; he teaches them to read.'

'But they're grown-ups!' exclaimed Poppy. 'They must be able to read.'

'Very surprising to me, like you. Frank says that some of the men are not educated.'

'I could read when I was five,' said Poppy.

'Yes. You are a clever girl. So your dad is being a teacher. And also he says he is going to the gym.'

'Dad in the gym!'

'That is surprising to me too. Your dad always say exercise is for the unfit and he is fit and strong.'

'What else did he write?' asked Poppy. She knew from her mum's manner that there was something not quite so good.

'It was a long letter, telling me many things. He even sees a priest on Sunday.'

'A priest?' exclaimed Poppy. Her dad had never been keen on church, saying that in Irish families, the women went to the church and the men went to the pub. He had come to her First Communion, though, and had given her a mother-of-pearl rosary he told her had belonged to his mother.

'Also,' Irena brightened, 'he is singing. There is a choir. I don't know properly. People come from outside. He has joined to please me, he said.'

'That's good,' Poppy had heard the story of Big Frank's beautiful singing voice often enough to know just how happy this piece of news would make her mum. 'So are you,' Poppy paused, 'are we going to visit him soon?'

A long silence followed this question. Poppy waited, frowning.

'He say no.' Irena mumbled, and bit her lip.

Poppy couldn't believe what she was hearing. It was all very well if she decided not to see her dad, but for him not to want to see her, his only daughter, his only child, seemed extraordinary.

'Just me?' she said in a self-pitying voice.

'No. Both you and me. He says it is too disturbing

to see us. He say he likes letters. He will write. He is sorry. He is very very sorry.'

Poppy thought about this. She thought about their last visit to the island. Then she remembered how she and Will had talked about 'The Rat Who Wanted to be Liked' instead of how to help her dad escape. If he didn't even want to see them, how could she get him off an island in the middle of nowhere?

'So what does he want us to do?' asked Poppy. 'Does he want us to forget all about him?' She knew this wasn't a very friendly thing to say, but she couldn't bear the idea of her mum going all miserable and murky again. What joy it had been swimming through the green sea waters in Cornwall! Everything had seemed so clean and clear.

'Your dad loves us very much,' said Irena. 'That is why it is difficult for him. He just sees us for an hour or two and then we are gone. I am sorry too,' she added. 'I think partly he is sparing us pain.'

'Oh, yes.' Poppy tried to sound agreeable but she thought she would never call her dad 'Big Frank' again. 'So do we just get on with our lives?' She couldn't keep the anger out of her voice.

'He wants us to be happy,' said Irena helplessly. 'You are a young girl so I don't tell you too much, but he is ashamed of what happens. He is a good man.'

'Of course he's a good man, because he's innocent,' said Poppy in a quiet voice.

Irena frowned, then leant over to take away her plate. 'Enough *blinis*?' She turned round again, her voice falsely cheerful. 'And this weekend we prepare for school. So much to be bought.' She looked at Poppy hopefully. 'And I have new students too. It seems parents have forgotten I have a husband in prison. Maybe they are mini Mozarts. We have much to keep us busy.'

'Yes. We do,' said Poppy, trying hard to be hopeful too. And actually, even if she did have an unloving dad in prison, she was looking forward to the new school term.

Chapter Twenty-Five

Poppy, Jude and Will walked together to school most mornings. They had to leave a littler earlier than usual to allow for Will's slow pace, although he insisted he was fine. Jude's mum said she'd drive them when it was too wet or cold.

One morning, Will quietly asked Poppy, 'Shall I tell Jude about Angel? About the police?'

'Why not?' Poppy frowned. Angel had been part of the Great Escape Plan, but that was all in the past. When she thought of her dad, she had an ugly, cross feeling. She listened as Will made Jude gasp with his description of Angel's arrest.

'A policeman holding both arms! How strong do they think he is?' Jude sounded so outraged that Poppy felt ashamed of her own lukewarm response, even if she suspected that it reflected more Jude's liking for drama than her liking for Angel.

'I think we should check he's OK,' said Will.

'He's not at school any more and we don't know where he lives,' pointed out Poppy.

'His dad went back into prison, didn't he?' said Will thoughtfully.

'You mean, we could catch him when he visits his dad?' Poppy could see that might work. 'On Saturdays. That's when his family go.' On the other hand, the thought of going anywhere near Her Majesty's Prison Grisewood Slops again made her uneasy.

Jude asked, 'How is Big Frank?'

Poppy frowned. The last thing she wanted was to explain that he'd stopped being Big Frank and had become a prisoner who looked after boring animals, taught very stupid men and sang, but didn't want anything to do with his wife or daughter.

Luckily, they arrived at the school gates.

'He's fine,' said Poppy, and neither Jude nor Will said another word.

It was a couple of weeks before they could all get together on a Saturday to visit Grisewood Slops. At the sight of the prison, Poppy began to shake. It made her realise just how much she'd hated going to visit her dad. He might be doing her a favour by not allowing visits to HMP Castlerock.

'I'll stay this side of the road,' she said. It was drizzling and they all had their hoods up.

'Do you remember when the white van with your dad inside nearly ran us over?' asked Jude.

'The sweat box,' said Poppy. But she didn't want to remember.

'And I was still in hospital,' added Will, 'waiting for your dad to arrive.'

'Drop it, can't you,' said Poppy.

At last the visitors began to pour out of the prison gates, putting coats on and umbrellas up. They wore the look of relief that Poppy recognised from her own visits. Rain, hail or storm – anything was better than being locked up behind high walls.

'There he is!' shouted Will, who'd already crossed the road. Poppy and Jude followed quickly.

Angel saw them at the last moment. He was carrying Gabriel.

'Hey,' said Angel.

'Bye!' shouted Gabriel, bending his chubby fingers.

'He can talk!' exclaimed Poppy.

'Bye. Bye. Bye.' shouted Gabriel proudly.

'Hi,' said Angel's mum. 'Your dad OK?'

'Fine,' said Poppy. 'Guess what? He's singing.'

Angel looked impressed. 'Hey, that's great, man.'

'How are you?' asked Jude, who was always direct when she wanted to know something. 'We heard—'

'Ssshh,' said Will.

Angel shifted from foot to foot, then frowned. Gabriel, who had stopped saying 'Bye,' frowned too. Poppy thought how alike they looked.

'Catch up with you outside school, shall I? *Your* school. I've left it.'

And they had to be content with that because he hurried off after his mum and Seraphina.

It was another week before Angel appeared again. Poppy spotted him lurking in a side road near the school. Jude and Will came out of the gate and followed her.

'So, hey.' Angel had a bicycle with him, not flashy and rather battered.

'Will saw you being arrested,' said Jude immediately.

Angel shrugged. 'Oh, that. I was nicked, wasn't I.'

He looked over his shoulder as if keeping a lookout for something.

'We're not going to stand on the street, are we?' Poppy felt embarrassed to be seen talking to him. 'It's cold,' she added hastily.

'We can't go to my house,' said Jude. 'My mum's there.'

'My mum's home too,' said Will awkwardly.

Poppy thought, neither of them want Angel in their house. He's too street for them.

'You can come to me,' she said. 'My mum will be back later. She won't mind.' In fact, her mum probably would mind, but she'd just have to accept Angel. He was a friend.

They walked in a group. Will and Jude told their mums they were going to Poppy's, and didn't tell them Irena was out – and certainly didn't tell them Angel was coming along.

It was odd sitting round the kitchen table, the four of them, like a meeting. Poppy got them juice and the remainder of the biscuits they'd brought back from Poland.

Jude and Will pronounced them delicious, but Angel looked at them with horror.

'Not my sort of thing,' he muttered. 'No offence.'

'None taken.' Poppy gave him a digestive instead. She thought she was doing well as a hostess.

'So, you got nicked?' said Jude, who'd been waiting for this moment.

'What's this? An interrogation? Had enough of that with the feds – police to you.' Angel pushed his chair back as if he might leave.

'Shut up, Jude,' said Will. He turned to Angel. 'We're your friends, aren't we?'

'Oh yeah?' Angel seemed unconvinced.

'I did see you with the police – feds. I expect they picked on you.'

'Yeah,' said Angel but Poppy suspected there was a lot of 'No' or 'Not really' in his reply.

'I thought so,' said Will.

'Yeah. Well, they picked on me because I'd nicked a couple of CDs from that stall in Portobello. Everyone does it. They're nicked in the first place. Like a chain of ownership. Recycling by another name, isn't it. Back of the lorry, the Bello and yours truly.'

There was a pause. Angel ate his biscuit with a self-righteous expression on his face.

'But the police grabbed you anyway,' said Poppy tentatively.

'It's their job, isn't it. Stupid stallholder called the

station, didn't he, and there was two feds coming right up the road.' He took another biscuit from the packet. 'It hasn't worked out so bad. They've sent me to this special school in the Bush. One-to-one teaching a lot of the time. First time anyone's cared. You should hear me read.'

Poppy, Jude and Will tried not to look at each other. They'd all been able to read for years and they were younger than Angel.

'I'm writing, too,' added Angel. 'Hey, did you ever finish that rat story? Seraphina still asks for it. ''Rat! Rat! Want Rat!'''

This was a relief. Now they could tell him about the publication and their visit to Ivy Underhill arranged for a fortnight's time. Poppy had found a copy of the story and read it aloud – and this was how Irena found them when she returned.

They all stood up guiltily – had they really finished all the biscuits – both sorts? Irena stared in surprise. She turned to Poppy.

'I thought you were going to Jude's?'

'I was.' Poppy faced her mum determinedly. 'Then we bumped into Angel, so we came here.' She paused. 'You remember Angel? My friend from the prison.'

Irena frowned, then seemed to make up her mind.

She even managed a smile. 'Hi, Angel. Family OK?'

'Not so bad.'

Irena turned to the stove and said in a slightly unnatural voice, 'Now, how about some good Polish soup?'

But everyone had to go, mumbling about homework and mums. At the door, Angel was pulling out his bike from the corridor, when he turned to Poppy. 'Know your dad's singing and all that, but if you need any help, whatever, you know, my dad's got connections right through the estate.'

Poppy blushed. She thought Angel understood more than anyone. 'The Great Escape, you mean?'

'Whatever,' repeated Angel.

'Thing is. . .' Poppy broke off.

'Got to go!' shouted Jude from the pavement. 'See you tomorrow.' Will had already left.

'Thing is,' Poppy began again. 'My dad doesn't want much to do with us. No visits.'

'Doing his bird the best way he knows.' Angel nodded wisely.

Poppy thought that sometimes Angel seemed much older than a schoolboy. 'Anyway, I think escaping from Castlerock would be just about impossible, unless you were a seagull.'

'Know what you mean. See you around, then.'

Poppy closed the door behind Angel. It seemed like the final final end of the Great Escape Plan.

Chapter Twenty-Six

Ivy Underhill's office was in a mews behind a big noisy road which went over a noisy railway line. Poppy, Will, Jude and Jude's mum, who had driven them there, wandered up and down the road for ages before they found the right turning. Jude was only there because she'd made such a fuss about *not* coming – but her mum had turned out to be useful.

'Magician Mews!' cried Poppy at last. They all thought it a wonderfully romantic address for a publisher. But a heavy downpour had exploded over their heads as Sally parked the car and now they were wet, tired and late.

The door was opened by a girl in enormously high heels at the end of exceptionally long thin legs. She peered down at them. 'Miss Underhill is expecting you.'

Jude stifled a nervous giggle and Will coughed.

They were shown into a large room whose walls were entirely covered with covers of children's books.

While they waited, Will, Poppy and Jude picked out the ones they'd read.

'Welcome!' A little round woman wearing green spectacles, striped jacket, a multi-coloured skirt and blue trainers came into the room. 'Oh, dear. You're soaking. Araminta didn't say. Take off your jackets at once and I'll get towels and hot chocolate.'

Right from that moment, the meeting wasn't at all as Poppy had expected. 'Unders', as Ivy Underhill told them to call her, hardly talked about the book, but asked them all about their lives. With their wet hair wrapped in warm towels and mugs of hot chocolate in their hands, all three children were soon confiding in her the kinds of things they'd never usually tell grown-ups.

'So you started writing the Rat in prison?' said Unders, looking over her green glasses with little bright blue eyes. She seemed all colour and kind curiosity.

'It was something to do,' explained Poppy. 'My dad suggested we did an alternative line story. Out loud first. Then we wrote it down. My dad's innocent, you know,' she added, almost without thinking.

'Of course he is, with a daughter like you,' agreed Unders understandingly.

'And my mum did the drawings,' continued Poppy.

Unders looked enquiringly at Jude's mum.

'Not me,' she said. 'I'm Jude's mum.'

'So you are.' Unders turned back to Poppy. 'But I haven't got your mum's drawings here?'

'They're Will's,' said Poppy. 'My mum only did a few, so when Will was recovering from his operation. . . .'

'Oh, yes.' Unders turned to Will, 'You're the one with the heart.'

The whole meeting was like that, one thing leading to another until Poppy felt Unders knew everything about them – even the Great Escape Plan which didn't work and Angel who had got nicked but perhaps it had all worked for the best because now he could read.

'I shall send his school some books,' Unders said, and made a little note on a pad she'd been using.

After an hour or so, she looked at her watch and said regretfully, 'If you're dry now, I'll have to let you go. Drop the towels in the corner.' So the children unwound their heads and collected their mugs into a tidy group on the table.

'Yes,' said Unders. 'Now we know each other, we can get on with Rat. I'll send you an edited version and a contract in the next few weeks. I am very glad to have made your acquaintance. Saving your presence' – and she smiled towards Jude's mum who had kept remarkably silent throughout – 'I find kids far more interesting and imaginative than us old things. I hear no contradictions.'

Suddenly raising her voice, she shouted, 'Araminta!'

In a moment Araminta tottered in and led them to the outside door. 'See you again, I expect,' she said from her great height, 'Unders took to you, I could tell that.'

'Well!' exclaimed Sally when they were outside. 'She wasn't very businesslike, was she?'

The children breathed deeply. The rain had passed, leaving a sunlit evening. Their heads felt light and airy without the towels. Poppy could feel her hair standing up and waving in the breeze.

'I liked her,' she said.

'That's good.' Sally took them back to the car. The big road seemed less noisy now. It was lined by huge trees from which leaves were floating gently down. One landed at Poppy's feet. It was large and flat and shaped like a hand.

Poppy bent down and picked it up. She laid it on

the palm of her own hand; it was much bigger – the size of Big Frank's hand, although she didn't call him that any more. She would have liked to have told him about Unders.

'Come on, Poppy!' called Jude's mum. 'Did I tell you I put a chicken and ham pie in the oven?'

Poppy was now almost used to living in a house with only her mum. Even though her dad's presence had never been very reliable, he'd always been expected and when he did come, everything was larger and more fun.

The days and weeks moved on quietly. She did send Frank letters now and again but they were fairly boring, saying things like, 'I was top in the history test today,' while his to her were so short as to be hardly letters at all. They said things like, 'I hope you're well,' and 'I'm very well.' But then Poppy supposed there wasn't much news where he was. He hadn't even commented when she told him a bit about Unders.

It was as if he didn't exist, now that he was in that faraway prison. In fact, it was hard to believe in the existence of HMP Castlerock on the top of its rocky island.

School was better. She was working hard again and getting high marks in all the subjects she liked. Will and Jude, although so completely different from each other, were her closest friends. About once a week Angel appeared at the end of the school day and they sloped off to Poppy's house. Irena was used to him now and told Poppy that he was 'a very courteous boy', which made them all laugh.

As autumn speeded up, so did the leaves, falling faster and faster from the trees. Often Poppy tracked the big ones to where they landed on the pavement. Sometimes, if one was an unusual colour, she would pick it up and take it home to her room. Soon she had quite a collection – red, gold, bronze, dark-green, lime-green, yellow, or a mix of several colours.

'They're beautiful!' Irena came into her bedroom and stared at the top of her chest of drawers where all the leaves were laid out.

'I like them,' said Poppy diffidently. She didn't tell her mum that they reminded her of hands. Especially she didn't tell her that they reminded her of her dad's hands. They were not talking about him at the moment.

'I'll tell you what,' suggested Irena. 'We could stick them on to a board. They would look lovely and they wouldn't curl up so quickly.' So they spent a happy evening together making patterns with the leaves on a large piece of cardboard and finally hanging it on the wall.

'There!' Irena stood back to admire their work. 'A masterpiece.'

Poppy looked at her mum. Her cheeks were pink, her hair loose round her face. She had taken on so many new students that two days ago she'd had the piano moved from Poppy's bedroom to the living room. 'It means I can teach here at home,' she explained to Poppy. 'Which mean more money.'

Poppy had been about to say, 'Dad will be furious!' when she realised that Dad wouldn't even know. She told herself she was glad her mum was busy, because the worst thing was when she was miserable and lonely. When Poppy felt lonely, she went up to her bedroom and wrote her diary.

The leaves hung where the piano had once stood. Poppy could see them from her bed and at night, when the only light came from a street lamp outside the window, they seemed even more like big hands reaching out towards her.

The weeks passed. There were no more leaves on the trees and it was already dark on the way home from school. Unders called them for another meeting and they began to make changes to the Rat. Otherwise nothing very important happened, unless you counted Irena announcing that she didn't think it worth making her special Polish Christmas pudding this year. But that was just sad.

Then one evening, Irena met Poppy at the school gates with a look of suppressed excitement.

'What is it, Mum? What's happened?'

'I'll tell you when we get home,' said Irena, and she walked with her head down as if to avoid temptation.

Chapter Twenty-Seven

'So?' asked Poppy, the moment they were through their front door.

'Follow.' Irena went into the kitchen.

Poppy saw there was an envelope on the table. Her mum took out a slip of paper from inside and slid it across to Poppy. 'It's an invitation,' she said.

Poppy read to herself:

THE GOVERNOR OF HMP CASTLEROCK

AND

THE TRUSTEES OF THE FOSSIL MUSICAL SOCIETY

INVITE YOU TO A SPECIAL PERFORMANCE OF

GUYS AND DOLLS

There was a time and date and an RSVP to an e-mail address.

Poppy looked up at her mother. Irena nodded. 'It surprised me too. It arrives three days ago. Then yesterday I had a letter from your dad. Everything is explained. He has a big part in the production. Some of the cast are professionals. Some from the prison. Your dad's voice is so good that he has a main part.' Irena's eyes shone. 'Have I not always told you he has a great voice. I am so proud!'

Poppy still couldn't think what to say? Did Dad want to see them now? After so many weeks? She knew she couldn't say it out loud without sounding angry and she didn't want to spoil her mum's excitement.

'There's more to know.' Irena came round and gave Poppy a hug. 'It's not just you and me who are invited. You can bring friends. We must e-mail all details for security. Birth certificates. They must find birth certificates. Oh, darling. At last something good. Not just work, and your dad so far away!'

Irena looked happily into Poppy's face. She knew she must say something, but it wasn't clear what. Did her mum really think Jude and Will and Angel (who spent too much time in prison visiting rooms anyway) would want to travel hundreds of miles to admire her dad's singing?

'They will love it, your friends! And afterwards I will treat you to fish and chips on the sea front.'

Irena's cheeks glowed as she pictured the occasion. 'What do you think, my darling?'

'It's fab,' said Poppy, adding in a mumble, as her mum still wore a questioning look, 'I'll talk to the others. They might be busy.'

'But it's weeks away,' said Irena. 'They'll have time to make plans.'

'I'll ask them tomorrow.' Poppy made a huge effort, which made her blush because really it was a lie. 'I'm very glad Dad's feeling better and wants to see us.'

'Yes,' agreed Irena fervently. 'This is a bright day.'

Poppy didn't tell any of her friends about the invitation for a while. Then she told Jude and Will as they stood in the playground, shivering together in the cold. Their reactions were exactly the opposite of what she had expected. Jude was wildly excited and Will, who'd always been so sympathetic, was doubtful.

'How odd,' he said, frowning. 'A musical in prison. I mean, where will they do it? They can't have a theatre.'

'What does it matter where it's done?' Jude broke

in. 'It'll be great to go and support Big Frank doing his thing.' She began to jump up and down, swinging her arms to keep warm.

'Do you think he really wants us there?' Will looked pale and small.

'That's what he wrote to my mum,' said Poppy. 'Angel too.'

'Angel?' exclaimed Jude.

'Of course, Angel,' said Will. He seemed to make up his mind. 'If Angel comes, I'll come too – if my mum lets me.'

Jude stopped jumping and looked concerned. 'I see what you mean. Although I think it's more my dad who would say no.'

Poppy frowned, and wound a bit of hair round her finger. It wasn't very nice to think that her friends might be forbidden to go and see her dad, wherever he was. For the first time, she felt keen to go herself.

'Well, I'm going, anyway,' she said fiercely.

'Of course *you're* going,' said Jude. 'Big Frank's your dad.'

Poppy looked at Will but he didn't say anything. She let go of her hair so it sprang upwards. 'This is the man who we tried to help escape from prison because he's INNOCENT!' She was shouting by the end.

'I'll ask my mum,' said Will in a subdued voice. 'I suppose I'm a bit frightened. Sorry.'

'At least you're honest!' Poppy's eyes flashed scornfully towards Jude, who'd started jumping again. She remembered all over again how horrible Jude had been when Frank first went into prison.

Jude stopped jumping. 'I'm sorry, too. I think I'm frightened as well. And I do think my dad might refuse to let me come with you.' She looked down at her shoes as if they'd suddenly become interesting. 'He's not very kind about people in prison.'

'My dad's *innocent*!' repeated Poppy. She couldn't think why she was suddenly defending her dad when she'd been so cross with him.

'I know.' Jude looked embarrassed. Luckily for her, the end of break bell rang. 'I'll ask,' she said. And they all went inside.

It was another few days before Angel appeared and Poppy could ask him. It was raining and both of them had their hoods up. She was on her own, waiting for her mum – who was late.

'Hey,' said Angel.

'Hi,' said Poppy.

'Won't need a shower tonight,' said Angel.

'Want to come home?' asked Poppy.

'Just stopping by. Good, are you?'

'Apart from my mum being late.' Poppy wondered if she should tell Angel then and there about the invitation from HMP Castlerock. Somehow it felt harder than asking Jude and Will. 'My mum's made some new cakes,' she said. 'English ones.'

'Hello, Angel.' Irena emerged from under an approaching umbrella. 'Coming back, are you? I've baked new cakes.'

'I've told him that,' said Poppy. She thought that sometimes Angel seemed like a wild animal you had to gently win over.

'Just for a bit, then. Got to babysit Gabriel and Seraphina, haven't I. Mum's working.'

They walked briskly back, not talking. Soon they were in the warm kitchen with sugared cakes and hot chocolate. (Ever since visiting Under's office Poppy had drunk a lot of hot chocolate.)

'I hope you're coming to hear Poppy's dad sing,' said Irena.

Angel looked blank. Blanker than blank, actually.

'I was just going to ask him, Mum,' said Poppy. 'The thing is, Dad's singing in a musical. . .' As she explained, she saw Angel's face change from surprised to wary to anxious, and back to surprised.

'You want *me* there?' he asked.

'Certainly,' said Irena. 'My daughter's friends are invited. We must get security clearance for those ten years and over.'

'Me,' said Angel.

'There you are,' agreed Irena.

Poppy could see that her mum had expected more enthusiasm. 'Angel has a lot of childcare to fit in,' she said.

Angel looked thoughtful. 'My dad was in one of those prison gigs. We all went along. He was helping with the stage managing – you know, lights and things – before they threw him out. He was found with a bit of . . . you know. We went along anyway, though. It wasn't bad. My dad's friend acted a pimp. Found it easy, didn't he.'

'Then you know all about it,' said Irena, in her determined-to-be-positive voice.

'Cheers,' said Angel – which was more positive than either Jude or Will.

To Poppy's surprise, Jude's parents and Will's mother

said they could go to the prison, and then Angel said he could go too. Poppy suspected he'd given himself permission, but he said his mum's sister was visiting, so she'd help with the children.

'There you are!' Irena clapped her hands when she heard the news. 'We'll have a lovely day out. I knew it would work out. '

Poppy wasn't so sure. The leaves on her wall had curled up and gone an ugly dark brown colour before dropping on the floor. She didn't think it was a good omen.

Then, with no warning, a railway strike was announced for the day of the performance.

'Oh, no. No! No!' Irena held her head in her hands and rocked to and fro.

Unable to comfort her, Poppy went up to her room. A little later she heard the phone ring.

'Poppy! Poppy!' Her mother called up to her. 'Come down quick.'

Poppy found her mum sitting at the piano playing one jolly Polish dance tune after another. 'Guess what! You remember the Lennie who gave us a lift to Blackmore Bay with husband in prison? Yes? She gives us a lift. All of us. She borrows a car with many seats and her son will drive. She has rung just now.

She is a good woman to think of us. All is well again. You see!' Irena ended with a triumphant run up the piano.

'Yes,' said Poppy, and hugged her mum and tried to forget that she'd been relieved they might not be able to go.

'Only four days,' murmured Irena, playing a slower and more romantic tune.

But two days later, Irena was back with her head in her hands. Outside the window, thick white snowflakes poured down from a leaden sky. The temperature was freezing. Outside London, it was even colder.

'England doesn't get cold like this,' Irena wailed to Poppy. 'This is Polish winter!'

'Not often,' agreed Poppy, who was at home because school had closed. She thought the snow was beautiful, and Jude's mum had promised to drive them to Hampstead Heath that afternoon so that they could toboggan down the slopes.

'I'll ring Lennie,' said Irena.

Poppy left the house while Irena was talking to

248

Lennie and when she got back, Irena had just had her fourth phone conversation with her.

'It will be OK,' she announced triumphantly. 'Lennie says forecast say that snow and ice come quickly and go quickly. Besides, she has a 4x4 car, good for all weather conditions. Tell to your friends. Their parents will want to know. Lennie's son is a driver by profession. We can all be safe and comfortable, whatever the weather, although weather will be good.'

'Yes, Mum,' said Poppy. Her face was burning from the hours she had spent dashing about in the snow.   Secretly, she was wondering whether something else – perhaps an earthquake – would stop them from watching her dad sing in Her Majesty's Prison Castlerock.

Chapter Twenty-Eight

On the first Saturday in December, Lennie, smartly dressed in a red trouser suit, appeared on Poppy and Irena's doorstep.

'Your coach awaits you, ladies and gentlemen.' She smiled at all the faces peering at her from the narrow hallway.

Encouraged by Irena, they'd dressed smartly in their own style. Irena had put her hair up and stuck a glittering comb in the side. Poppy was wearing an embroidered skirt brought back from Poland. Jude wore a slinky lurex top. Will had a green shirt (which Poppy privately thought turned his pale complexion green too) and Angel sported a shiny black tracksuit which was so baggy, it looked as if it might fall right off him at any minute.

'Aren't we fine!' said Lennie as they bundled into the large black people-carrier.

'Hi, there, and welcome!' Lennie's son, Bernard, waved from the front seat. He was broad-shouldered, with a shaven head above a thick cable-knit sweater. Lennie sat beside him, Irena behind her, Jude and Will beside her and Poppy and Angel in the back row.

Despite Poppy's misgivings, it was hard not to feel excited. Outside, it was still cold and there were lumps of greyish snow on the pavement. Poppy thought of the steep winding road up to the prison. She couldn't imagine them making it to the top, even if they were in a 4x4.

Angel nudged her. 'Some car!'

'Do you think it can go over snow and ice?'

'Course it can. Did you see the size of its wheels?'

Poppy hadn't. She left that sort of thing to boys. So it seemed another reason for not getting to Castlerock had been overcome.

'Comfortable back there?' Lennie called from the front.

'Very comfortable, thank you,' they all replied.

They were soon on the outskirts of London. A tape of *Kaiser Chiefs* blared out cheerily from six speakers.

'There's more snow out here.' Irena was staring anxiously out of the window.

Poppy, who was sitting directly behind her, touched her shoulder. 'It'll be OK, Mum. Angel says this tank will go through anything.'

'Thank you, my darling.' Irena gave her a smile.

When they were deep in the countryside, Bernard pulled in at a service station. 'Toilets, coffee-break, petrol and stretch your legs,' he announced.

They all climbed out and then returned quickly for hats and scarves. An icy wind blew in vicious gusts.

'It's freezing.' Jude shivered theatrically. 'I'm stretching my legs in the car.'

As they set off again, Irena looked up at the sky. Although it was mid-morning, it was as dark as if night was falling. 'I'm afraid there's snow up there,' she said to Bernard. He shrugged.

They drove on. All the cars had their headlights on. But Bernard put on a tape of Christmas carols and although Lennie complained it was too early in December for carols, they sang lustily, sometimes using the wrong words and not exactly in time.

At one point, Irena clapped her hands over her ears. 'I hope Frank sing better than this,' she moaned – and everyone burst out laughing.

Meanwhile, the threatening sky seemed to drop lower and lower. Then it became tinged with a sinister yellow glow.

'Do you think it's the end of the world?' asked Jude dramatically.

'Nothing like.' Will gave her a shove.

'Nonsense,' said Lennie firmly. 'You kids haven't seen *real* weather. When I lived in Oklahoma we endured tornadoes on a regular basis. Called them 'twisters' because they could take off the head of a tree like it was a bottletop. Think Wizard of Oz.'

The snow began just as they reached the road that led into Blackmore Bay. Strong winds blew it sideways across the car.

'Are you all right, Bernard?' asked Irena nervously.

'Like my mother says, ten years growing up in the US of A gave me a handle on weather. We're just fine, Mrs Maloney.'

'Call me Irena,' said Irena in a small, I'm-trying-to-be-brave voice.

Blackmore Bay was already turning white, but the great stretch of sea remained a dark, glassy green.

'Look,' said Will, pressing his nose to the window pane, 'it's as if the sea is eating up the flakes of snow.'

They all watched as the thick white flakes hit the surface of the water and disappeared.

'I'm glad I'm not on one of those boats,' exclaimed Jude. They were passing the harbour where the rows of moored boats were even whiter than usual.

'What a buzz,' Angel whispered enthusiastically, 'to go out to sea in a snowstorm!'

Poppy didn't answer. She was waiting for the moment when they'd see the long causeway and ahead of it the steep cliffs of the island. It had been forbidding enough on a summer's day. She peered anxiously round her mum's shoulder.

They arrived at the causeway quite suddenly; one minute they were travelling on a snowy road with houses on either side, the next, there was just the sea. The murky atmosphere reflected in the water and turned it black.

'The island's ahead,' Poppy told Angel, who pressed his face against the window.

Bernard had turned off the music and, as they reached the centre of the causeway, the only sound was the wind whistling and screeching across their car. Flurries of snow burst against the windows.

'Where is it? The prison, I mean?' asked Jude in a trembly voice.

'Ladies and gentlemen,' said Lennie in the same loud voice she'd used to announce her arrival at the house. 'We see ahead of us the famous nineteenth century prison of Castlerock at the topmost point of the famous and ancient Castle Island. Abandon hope, all ye who enter here!' Then she laughed. But no one else did.

'They won't get much of an audience, will they,' said Irena. 'Not in this weather.'

'Most of them are up there anyway,' pointed out Bernard. 'Locked in.'

'People living round here are tough,' added Lennie. 'And bored. And curious. They'll show up for a convict production.'

Convict, thought Poppy. What an odd word for her dad.

They drove off the far end of the causeway and on to the island. A few minutes more and they were travelling along the winding road that led up to the prison.

'I can't see it anywhere,' said Will, craning his neck from one side to another.

'It's above our heads,' Poppy whispered to Will, 'You won't see it now till we get there.' She noticed that everyone had gone quiet.

'We'll get up there all right,' muttered Bernard to Lennie. 'But if it freezes, we'll have a right old time getting down without skidding over the edge.'

'Sshh.' Lennie shut him up quickly. 'Everything will be fine.'

The car churned slowly upwards. On either side, great banks of windswept snow grew even higher. Then above them appeared the huge stone walls that had so frightened Poppy before.

'We're nearly there,' she told Angel.

'Beats Grisewood Slops for house of horror atmosphere, doesn't it?' Angel didn't seem at all shocked. Maybe it made a difference if it wasn't your dad locked inside.

Then the tunnel closed over their heads. Jude gave a frightened yelp.

'Made it!' shouted Lennie, as they came out the other side. Amazingly, there were quite a lot of other cars parked already – mostly jeeps and 4x4s. 'See,' added Lennie, 'country folk don't turn tail at a few specks of snow.'

The snow was lighter, but it was bitterly cold as they bundled out of the car and went across to the visitors' centre. Snow clung to its roof. High above it the enormous walls, outer and inner, rose into the sky, the snow turning even the barbed wire white.

Poppy took her mum's hand. 'OK, Mum?'

'I just want to see your dad.'

Poppy wished it felt as easy for her. She glanced at Will and Jude who were staying close together. She thought they were trying to repress shivers – but not from cold.

The visitors' centre was hot and filled with people, including half a dozen children. Lennie had already found a friend and was chatting animatedly. The heat inside and the ice cold air outside had combined to fog over the windows so that they couldn't see out.

'Look at that!' exclaimed Angel excitedly, as a huge lump of snow slid off the roof and exploded on the ground.

A prison officer, tall and confident, came in with a clipboard. He began to check off their names.

'Special treatment, isn't it,' commented Angel, who seemed to be enjoying himself. 'Now let's see about security.'

Angel, Poppy, Jude and Will did what they were told and took their coats over to the locker. Angel seemed to have become their leader.

'If your dad's Al Capone, then you know about the inside of prisons.' Will joked. Angel smiled, as Jude asked, 'Who was Al Capone?'

'Gangster in Chicago,' answered Will. 'Killed loads of people.'

'My dad's not a killer,' said Angel. 'Robbery with violence is the worst he ever did. Had to carry a gun, didn't he. Don't mean he planned to use it.'

Poppy had never heard Angel talk about his dad's offence before. Even if he hadn't hurt anyone, it seemed really bad to her. Judging by Will's and Jude's shocked faces, they thought so too. She was glad her dad was innocent.

'Drugs. That's my dad's main line of business,' Angel added, raising his voice.

'Sshh,' said Poppy's mum, who'd just joined them. She looked at the guard nervously.

'Sorry, Mrs. Maloney.' Angel shuffled his feet guiltily.

After a while they were gathered into groups of ten and shepherded inside the prison proper.

Poppy had hoped security might not be as bad as before, since this was a special event. But the opposite was true: shoes off, bodies patted down, mouths searched, dogs sniffing, and through the metal detector. Even then, several men and women and even children were taken off to be searched more thoroughly in separate cubicles.

'Sometimes they even take off Gabriel's nappy,' commented Angel, watching them go.

Then it was into the 'air-lock' before allowing the dogs – which were black Labradors – to give them a good sniff. Jude automatically put her hand down to pat one and got a ticking-off from one of the guards: 'They're not here to socialise, you know.' Jude took her hand away quickly.

At last they were through security and waiting in another room. Angel whispered confidentially, 'See, they're looking for drugs and mobile phones, but most of that stuff's brought in by the screws, anyway.'

'Is that so?' Jude seemed to have got over the shock and gone back to her usual curious self.

'Not here,' hissed Poppy. Will nodded. It was best that Al Capone's son kept his mouth shut for the moment.

When all the visitors had arrived in the waiting room, an officer announced that they would now be taken to the prison chapel where the performance was to be held. 'You'll get a chance to talk to your relatives and friends over tea and biscuits after the show.'

Once more, they were divided into groups of ten and led out across the open central space which Poppy remembered from before. Now it was white, although criss-crossed with large dark foot-prints. She looked up at the sky, uncomfortably close, and not a seagull to be seen.

The officer in the front was a jovial woman who clapped her hands together and told those nearest to her, 'You're in for a treat. I saw it yesterday. Couldn't believe my eyes. Might have been in the West End. Mind you, the work they've put in!'

Lennie, who was just behind her, nodded happily and even Poppy's mum managed a smile.

'It isn't the full version,' continued the officer chattily, 'or we'd be here till midnight.'

'What is the show, then?' asked Angel.

Poppy realised that she hadn't thought once about what they were going to see. All she'd thought about was meeting her dad, after so many months of rejection. '*Guys and Dolls*,' she said.

'That's it,' said the jovial officer. 'You wait till you hear Sky Masterton blasting it out. Quite a voice, that one. Now then, one more set of keys and we're in the promised land. Front seats reserved for Governor and guests, the rest of you anywhere.'

The keys turned noisily; one heavy iron door, then another was pushed creakingly open and suddenly they were out of the dim cold and in a warm, bright, high-ceiling space. At one end was a stage, while the rest of the room was filled with plastic chairs. Behind the stage was a huge painting of the New York City skyline.

'Hey!' exclaimed Angel. 'Guess this is my first visit to a theatre. Funny it should be in a prison.'

A big man stands on a brilliantly lit stage. He is wearing a flashy striped suit and a broad tie, luminously turquoise and yellow. His red hair is parted and plastered down. He is standing with a pretty woman dressed in the sober uniform of the Save a Soul Mission.

The man begins to sing to her. It's four o'clock in the morning in New York City. He's a high-rolling gambler and his name is Sky Masterton.

In real life he is Big Frank.

Sarah Brown, the Save a Soul soldier, joins in the singing as the two declare their love for each other.

The sentimental scene is broken up as a stream of gamblers burst out from the mission house where they've been enjoying an all-night poker game. They are, in no particular order, Nicely Nicely Johnson, Benny Southstreet and Rusty Charlie, Harry the Horse, Nathan Detroit and Big Julie, a hulk from Chicago nursing a bad temper and a snub-nosed revolver. They are all wearing wide-shouldered gangster suits, broad ties and wide-brimmed hats, and they talk out of the sides of their mouths with thick accents.

They sing and dance and crack jokes. Their big problem is how to find a safe place for their high-rolling

game. At the centre of their story is Sky Masterton.
Will he carry on a lifetime of gambling and thuggery —
or will he be converted by the virtuous Sarah Brown to a
different way of life?

Chapter Twenty-Nine

Poppy sat among her friends in the middle of the audience. She decided to stop being surprised or worried and just enjoy herself. Now and again she looked along the row to her mum's face, which seemed to wear a permanent smile.

The surprising thing was that, although they were inside a prison, they were having a wonderful time. Poppy knew Angel felt the same, because he kept whispering things like, 'Wow!' 'Where are we, man?' 'Cool.' 'Where *are* we?'

Jude and Will weren't so surprised, because they'd never been in prison before and didn't know what to expect. When they whispered, it was about her dad: 'I didn't know he could *act*!' from Jude. 'Your dad's the best thing in the show by far!' from Will.

Around them, the audience – a mixture of prisoners, officers, family, and friends – laughed, clapped and cheered on the soloists.

'Your dad's so handsome!' whispered Jude.

For a moment Poppy closed her eyes. She pictured those days which seemed years ago now, when Big Frank had lived at home and used to pick her up from school. He was always the centre of attention, recognised by all her friends as a very special kind of dad. When he didn't arrive, they'd ask disappointedly, 'Where's Big Frank?' as if he was a celebrity or film star.

Now he was a star again. Poppy opened her eyes. The show was coming to an end. Sky Masterton was making his way round the stage beating the big bass drum of the Save a Soul Mission. He had given up criminal life for love of Sarah Brown. The whole cast began to sing a number called 'Happy Endings', with Sky in the middle.

Then they were all bowing and the audience stood up and clapped and shouted and whistled, determined to show just how much they'd enjoyed it.

'Even the screws are clapping,' said Angel in amazed tones.

The cast was joined on stage by the director of the production and she was joined by the director of the musical society who'd put on the show. Then they were joined by the Governor. He praised everybody, 'especially the men who'd never before opened their mouths except to fill them.'

This got a bit of a laugh and a few ironic cheers. Someone shouted 'Music!' So the Governor went back to his seat and the man who'd played the synthesiser appeared, followed by the man on the drum set and the man on the electric guitar. There was more cheering and a few prisoners stamped on the floor.

As the noise rose, Poppy noticed a forward movement from the prison officers standing at the side of the chapel. It reminded her unpleasantly where they were. Then it was all celebration again.

The lights came up among the audience. Lennie hugged Irena. 'He was ab fab, my dear. A real star!'

And Jude and Will took turns to say to Poppy, 'Your dad was the best thing in it!'

'You can tell him yourself,' said Poppy, embarrassed by so much praise, even if it was for her dad. The performers were coming off the stage into the audience. Meanwhile, prisoners and screws were clearing away the chairs and setting up tables. Juices, a tea urn, sandwiches and biscuits were carried in from outside.

Big Frank came slowly, almost shyly, towards Poppy and her mum. He hugged them both. Irena had tears in her eyes.

'Did good, did I?'

'You know you did,' said Poppy proudly. She'd never seen her dad shy like this before. She pushed forward Jude and Will and Angel. 'They all thought you were terrific, too.'

'A long way for you to come.' Big Frank shook all their hands. 'You know, they always say an actor is only as good as his director, but I think the audience is what really matters.'

So they told him again and again just how cool he was, until he held up his hands in protest. 'I can feel my head swelling by the minute. How about sampling those biscuits I can see over there? Long time since I've seen a festive array like that.'

'Well, it's not long till Christmas,' said Lennie, coming over with her son and husband who, of course, Frank knew already since he was a prisoner too.

'Wise old Bob,' said Frank, clapping him on the shoulder, 'kept off the stage and on the lighting board. It's him I have to thank for my share of the spotlight.'

'My pleasure.' Bob bowed jokily. He looked remarkably like an older version of his son, with the same shaved head, except that he had a scar down one side of his face. 'Couldn't have highlighted a fitter lad, could I.'

At which point, they all took off for the biscuits, which were disappearing at an alarming rate. 'Not your usual prison fare,' said Angel knowingly.

Poppy frowned. Amid all the excitement she couldn't quite forget that her dad was in prison, and he shouldn't be, because he was innocent. That's what she'd always thought. She stared at his cheery, beaming face. At that moment he looked up too, and caught her eye.

He came over. 'All right, Pops, darling?' His blue eyes beamed at her lovingly.

Poppy took a deep breath. If she didn't ask him now, she never would. She glanced round; no one was near them.

'What is it?' asked Big Frank, still smiling. 'Would you like another orange juice?'

'Dad,' Poppy hesitated, gulped, 'Dad, did you really do what they say you did? The reason you're in prison. Did you really do something very bad? Or are you innocent, like I think? I need to know, Dad, I really do.'

As Poppy was speaking, Frank's expression changed. Now he was absolutely serious. He took her hand. 'Oh, Poppy. My own Pops. You're right. I do have to tell you. I owe you that. I've been cowardly. I've been ashamed. . .'

Poppy began to suspect what was coming. One part of her wanted to scream and put her hands over her ears. But even more, she knew she needed the truth. 'Tell me, Dad.'

Big Frank began slowly, pausing between each short sentence as if he had to make an effort with every word. 'It was about money. I wasn't earning. Lost my job. Years ago, long before I met your mum, I'd been involved with bad people. Spent time inside.'

'Inside!' Poppy whispered, horrified. 'You've been in prison before?'

Frank nodded miserably. 'I was only a lad. Led astray. But I should have known better, once I had your mum and you. I just thought of the money. I thought I'd buy you things. . .'

'Oh, Dad.'

'It was hard, your mum earning what money we had. No excuse, though. I should never have done it, for every reason in the world. Worst of all, it put me in here. Left you two alone.' Frank's voice faltered to a stop.

'What did you do?' This was the question she'd never dared ask her mum.

'I smuggled drugs. I'm a drug smuggler. A failed drug smuggler.' Frank bowed his head. 'Caught the first time I was out. Customs had a tip-off. What a fool! How stupid can you be!' He lifted his head and looked directly at Poppy. 'Oh, my darling, can you ever forgive me?'

Poppy wouldn't look at him. Her hero – a drug smuggler!

'So you're not innocent at all. You're guilty.' She said the word 'guilty' loudly and clearly.

Frank winced. 'Yes.' He paused before saying again, 'Can you ever forgive me? Or, if you can't do that, love me a little?'

Poppy thought about this. Children shouldn't have to forgive their dads. It shouldn't be like this. Then she thought how she'd hung on to the idea that Big Frank was innocent even when everything pointed to his guilt. She'd wanted him to be innocent because she loved him. But could she love him now he'd confessed that he was guilty?

She felt muddled and anxious. Still avoiding her dad's eyes, she turned, and immediately saw her mum. Irena was watching them both, her eyes filled with love. She must have been through the same feelings when she'd found out that her special, wonderful husband was guilty. Probably, Poppy guessed, she'd known it from the moment he was arrested. Probably he'd told her. But she still loved him. That was obvious.

'I'm so sorry. I'm so terribly, terribly sorry.' Poppy's dad squeezed her hand. 'If I could change anything, I would. I regret what I did every day. If you can't forgive me or love me, I won't blame you. I don't deserve it.'

At last Poppy looked at him. 'The thing is, Dad, if I'm honest, I think I've known you weren't innocent for ages. I was pretending to myself. I kept on about it so much just because I couldn't face the truth. Now I can. I've got to. But I'm not going to stop loving you. And, whatever you do, you'll always be my hero.'

'Oh, Poppy.' For a horrible moment, Poppy thought her dad was going to burst into tears. Luckily, at that moment they were suddenly surrounded by Irena and Will and Angel and Lennie and Bernard and Bob, all still celebrating Big Frank's brilliance.

'Hogging the star's forbidden, Poppy,' said Lennie.

Poppy watched her dad and saw that he was trying

hard to be a star again. She thought, he's guilty, which means he's bad, but he's also a star and my dad who loves me.

She felt she'd grown up so much in the last five minutes that if she lived until she was a hundred, she couldn't be any wiser.

'Screws getting ready to clear us out, aren't they.' Angel, who was standing by her, pointed at the guards.

Poppy looked up. The prison officers had a less relaxed look about them. They were gathering the prisoners together by a door at the other end of the room where the visitors had come in.

'Sad, isn't it.' Angel looked at Big Frank. 'So much excitement, then off we go, and your dad's left behind.'

Poppy watched Big Frank too. She could see the shadow growing behind his cheerfulness. 'But he's *guilty*.'

'What!' Angel stared at her in astonishment, 'You always said he was innocent. That's why we were going to help him escape.'

'Well, he isn't.' Poppy nearly smiled at the expression on Angel's face. 'He told me himself. I asked him and he told me.' She paused, before continuing. 'You always knew he was guilty, didn't you?'

Angel was too confused to answer. 'Aren't you mad at him?'

'Are you mad at your dad?'

Angel reflected. 'No point, is there. That's the way he is.'

'That's just how I feel,' said Poppy, although secretly she thought Angel's dad was much worse than hers.

'Didn't choose them, did we.' Angel's mood was beginning to lighten. 'At least we've got dads, haven't we? Not like Will. You'll see. Your dad will be in an open prison soon enough, and then it'll be home visits and telling you and your mum how you're doing everything wrong. When my mum's freaked by it all, she says the law's doing her a favour locking up my dad.'

'Hey, you two.' Lennie tapped Angel on the shoulder. 'You don't want to miss saying goodbye, do you?'

It was bad, the saying goodbye. Everyone was upset and trying to be brave. Poppy's dad said goodbye to each of his visitors in turn and thanked them for coming. Then he told Poppy, 'If you can't have a good dad, you'd better have good friends. And I can see you've got them.'

'Oh, Dad!' Poppy threw herself into his arms.

The prisoners were escorted away. Big Frank didn't look back, although they watched until he left the room. Only then were the visitors allowed to leave, once more gathered into groups of ten.

Chapter Thirty

Holding her mum's hand and with her friends all around, Poppy crossed the wide open area outside the chapel. It was no longer snowing and the sky was darkening as evening fell.

'The snow's melting,' said Bernard from behind. 'We'll have no problem getting back.'

For a moment they all stopped and looked upwards. Everywhere looked peaceful.

'Look at that!' Poppy whispered.

Ahead of them a pale moon, so slender and silvery it hardly seemed real, was rising above the great stone walls.

'A new moon,' Poppy's mum spoke in a hushed voice.

'Awesome,' said Will.

'Looks like a smile on its side,' said Angel

Poppy thought of Big Frank, by now locked up in his cell. Then she thought, he must have a window, and he'd see out of it the same glittering moon that they were looking at.

Suddenly Jude clapped her hands, 'Let's wish to the new moon!' she cried. 'Bow, turn round three times and make a wish.'

In a flash, they were all solemnly bowing and turning. The guards watched them, too amazed, perhaps, to hurry them forward.

'Now, wish!' cried Jude.

They stood quite still in a row and stared at the shining moon.

Poppy shut her eyes. 'I wish,' she said inside her head, 'that my mum and dad and me carry on loving each other, even though my dad's guilty and in prison.' Then she added in a bit of a rush, because the guards were closing in, 'And that Angel and Jude and Will and me carry on having adventures even if we can't get my dad out of prison.'

'Come on, now. We haven't got all night!' A booming voice broke up the ceremony. Quietly they filed across the open space and out through the prison walls.

Poppy's Hero is Rachel Billington's fifth
novel for children. She has also published
twenty adult novels, the latest, *The Missing Boy*,
about a thirteen-year-old who runs away
from home. Rachel has been an editor and
regular contributor to Inside Time, the national
newspaper for prisoners, since it was founded
over twenty years ago. Insights arising from
her prison work emerge in this new
childrens' novel. She has four children
and five grandchildren,
all keen readers.

SEA OF TEARS

Floella Benjamin

Jasmine is a typical British-born south London girl –
smart, independent, plenty of attitude. But her
parents are worried sick about the dangerous society
in which they are raising their precious only
daughter. They are determined to move the family
to Barbados for a quieter, safer life. Jasmine is
devastated – and when she starts school on the island
she is treated as an unwelcome outsider. All she
can think about is finding a way to get back to
Britain – and that's when she spots
the empty motor yacht. . .

'She writes with a sharp eye for details, with humour,
with justice, with passion and with hope.'
Julian Fellowes, writer and actor